THE MASTER OF THE CHEVRON

SAINT CUTHBERT TRILOGY BOOK 3

JOHN BROUGHTON

*ABOVE: Durham Cathedral:
the nave in 1841 looking east,
from Billings* PLATE XLI.

temporibus idest anno dominicae
Incarnationis· dc ·v· beatus papa
Gregorius postquam sedem roma
nae et apostolicae ecclesiae· xiii·
annos menses sex et dies decem glo
riosissime rexit defunctus est
atq· ad aeternam regni caelestis
sedem translatus· De quo nos bon

The Master of the Chevron is dedicated to <u>Anyone who loves English Cathedrals</u>

Special thanks go to my dear friend John Bentley for his steadfast and indefatigable support. His content checking and suggestions have made an invaluable contribution to
The Master of the Chevron

Frontispiece is by Dawn Burgoyne, with scholarly help from the ASHL group, special thanks to Helen M Cameron, Marie Hilder, Stella Mengels and Joseph St John.
Based on the St Petersburg Bede copied in the twin monastery of Wearmouth and Jarrow late 8th- early 9th century.

Dawn Burgoyne, medieval re-enactor/presenter specialising in period scripts. Visit her on Facebook at dawnburgoynepresents.

ONE

QUARRYMEN EKE OUT ROCK THAT HAS LAIN UNDISTURBED FOR millennia. The stonemason, blow by blow, creates an edifice destined to last as long. Decisions sculpt men's destinies. Their decisions, too, are shaped by experience, which lays character stone by stone and as long as the foundations are on solid rock, the man grows tall and straight.

Kenrick held out his large calloused hands, palms uppermost for scrutiny.

"The only weapons these hands have wielded, Edwy, are a stone chisel and a mallet. I must leave the fighting to you."

Edwy Aellasson glared at his younger brother. If the revolt was going to be a success, they needed every able-bodied man they could muster against the Norman invaders. William, who liked to style himself the Conqueror, may have won a decisive battle at Hastings against Harold, the true Saxon king of England, but the war was not over by any means, especially here in the far north of the kingdom. Kenrick was built like an ox and Edwy was determined to ensure that his brother's muscles were used in the just cause of defending the family estates against the foreigners. Edwy was a nobleman, an ealdorman, and he meant to throw in his lot with Edmund Ironside's grandson the Aetheling Edgar and any other trueborn Englishman, or even Dane, prepared to fight the Normans.

The thought that his brother, two years his junior, all brawn and no brain, it seemed, was not disposed to use his considerable physical strength on their behalf made his blood pound at his temples. Had the oaf lived among the Normans for too many years? What was he saying now?

"My cause is not yours, Edwy. I work for the glory of God. I am a mason, not a warrior. As I told you, I have no more interest in horse-trading or fighting. These last nine years I have used these hands to create, not to destroy."

Edwy scowled at his sibling and did not attempt to disguise the bitterness in his voice,

"Ay, working in Normandy, on behalf of the foe, who will stop at nothing to deprive Saxons and Anglians, of their hard-won and legitimately held lands. Would you turn against your family, brother?"

Kenrick sighed in exasperation,

Why should I fight for estates I have no share in? Why revolt against those who would promote my career?

This last thought was his closely guarded secret that he was unprepared to divulge even to his brother. As far as he was concerned, the discussion was over. He would make his way, as arranged, to Bishop Ethelwin in Durham and take up his position as Master Mason.

"May God protect you, brother, I am no warrior and I must leave you now to use my hands in the Lord's service."

"Traitor! May your God judge you harshly for betraying your people and your family! Go! Run off to your Norman masters but never return here calling yourself the son of Aella. Father will be turning in his grave at your faithlessness!"

Kenrick slammed the door, leapt on his grey dappled mare and wiping a tear from his eye, rode for Durham. His homecoming had not been as expected after nine years away in Normandy. The loving friendship and brotherliness enjoyed in his childhood and youth had been replaced by hatred and incomprehension and all thanks to lust for power and wealth—two things that did not interest him in the slightest. He had failed to communicate what truly motivated him to his brother and, yet, his was a family that could trace itself back to close friendship with Saint Cuthbert through a direct ancestor who bore his father's name, Aella. That particular Aella, the creator of the cover to the Cuthbert Gospel and the author of the *Vita Sancti Cuthberti* would surely have understood his, Kenrick's, desire to create a cathedral. But what did his brother know of his sibling's achievements in Normandy? How could he, a warrior, horse-breeder and owner of farmland, understand the essence of raising a stone monument destined to endure through the ages on a scale worthy of the Almighty? Had he not returned to Northumbria expressly for this purpose and did he not bear in his saddlebag a sealed letter that would make him the *master mason* of the new project in Durham?

At the gates of the city, high on its hill in a bend of the River Wear, guards barred his way but a glimpse of that seal was enough to allow his entry. He rode to the bishop's palace, paid a lad to look after his horse and used the impressed wax crest to gain admittance to Bishop Ethelwin's presence.

The prelate, a thin-faced man with grey hair and slightly hooked nose, a clergyman of austere aspect, broke the sigil and perused the writing with his intense piercing blue eyes. At last, he looked up and concentrated them on Kenrick.

"So, my son, you are a skilled mason and are designated to take charge of the building of the new cathedral. Come with me, I will show you the site."

The bishop led him out of the house not far towards the cathedral, upon which Kenrick gazed in astonishment.

"But Your Grace, there is *already* a cathedral here in Durham!"

"Ay, and it is new enough...but the king wishes a more glorious edifice to be raised right next to it. There are many considerations to take into account. In the first place, work is due to begin on a cathedral at Canterbury and I have it on good authority that the length of the church will be eighty-five paces of a tall man. Therefore, our new building must be longer, at least one hundred and twenty." The prelate's face glowed with enthusiasm—or was it fanaticism? "After all," he added, "this edifice will contain the shrine of Saint Cuthbert, and thus, it must be as grandiose as your skill can make it, my son."

"What about the Saxon building?"

"You may count on using the stone in your construction."

"So, it will be demolished. But the material will not suffice."

The bishop smiled knowingly and his expression became serious.

"I spoke with the mason who created this building and although he is an old man now, his mind is still acute. He tells me that across the river," the bishop pointed, "over yonder, there is a sandstone outcrop. The rock is of fine quality and ideal for masonry." The prelate looked smug.

Kenrick did not share that sentiment as he gazed in dismay across the deep gorge to the west bank of the fast-flowing Wear. The crag in question was only seven hundred yards as the crow flies but the drop of forty yards to the river made for inclines too steep for ox teams to convey the blocks of stone.

Kenrick made this point but the clergyman was prepared for the objection:

"By making a track north from the future quarry, and then east to cross the river on a wooden bridge, which we must begin building immediately at a place called Framwell, the gradients will be quite possible to manage with ox-drawn carts."

"I shall have to inspect the riverbed at the place you suggest, Your Grace."

The prelate was informed about this, too.

"You will find that the bed is rocky and the river shallow there, so its suitable for a bridge."

Kenrick smiled and scratched behind an ear with his forefinger,

"I see you have thought much about the whole business, for, naturally, we will have to support the wooden bridge on masonry piers and abutments, thus the riverbed will need to provide sound foundations."

"On the morrow, you will inspect the river at that place, in person. With your approval, work on the bridge will begin."

Walking back to the bishop's residence, Kenrick's head was awhirl with calculations of tonnes of dressed stone, weights of rubble needed and the question of the provision of limestone and sand. He knew from Normandy that an army of men would be required to work on a construction of this scale. But first, they had to beat flat a haul road, construct the bridge and make lime kilns for mortar production. All of this could only be achieved in times of peace. Yet, after visiting his brother, he knew of the threat of war.

I cannot betray Edwy! But there's a cathedral to be built.

The bishop cut across his musings by talking about Saint Cuthbert.

"Of course, you know the tale of how the saint came to choose Durham, do you not?"

Kenrick admitted he did not.

"Well, the monks, not for the first time, had to flee from the Vikings and leave Cuneceaster. Carrying his coffin, they followed two milkmaids who were searching for a dun-coloured cow and found themselves on this peninsula at this loop in the river. Thereupon, Cuthbert's coffin became immovable, which the monks took as a sign that the new shrine should be located here."

Kenrick was not thinking of the Viking raids of 995 but more modern warriors including his brother, Edwy. If he did not warn the bishop of the rebels' plans, their scheme for a new cathedral would be worthless.

———

Six months earlier,
Jumièges, Normandy, 1067 AD
The stonemasons assembled in a compact and jubilant group, the

moment they had been awaiting in the months leading up to the consecration of their masterpiece, the Abbey of Jumièges, had arrived. Today, William the Bastard, or as he preferred, William the Conqueror, after his successful enthronement as King of England was present at the ceremony. Talking about England, one blond-haired member of their group, known to them as *Le Saxon*, real name Kenrick Aellasson, had more reason than any of them to feel proud. He had reinvented himself as a mason, whilst still managing to continue the family tradition of horse-trading when called upon. As the second son, therefore with no likelihood of inheriting the estates in Northumbria, he had followed a natural curiosity and interest that had led him to the building site of the abbey to seal friendship with the master mason, Robert de Morlaix, who commanded an army of workmen that included carpenters, layers, metal-smiths, carriers, rope makers, and even animals—oxen: a marvellous bustling world apart, beguiling to Kenrick. He had discovered a universe into which he had plunged heart and soul, working hard to complete a seven-year apprenticeship and serving another two as a fully-fledged stonemason in his own right.

An archbishop, the abbot, priors, priests and deacons marched in procession in order of ecclesiastical rank, the senior prelate sprinkling holy water from his aspergillum and catching Kenrick full in the face, making him feel even more blessed. He gazed at the richly bejewelled processional cross, its bearer one step ahead of the archbishop, and copied its form, signing with his hand over his chest.

The masons had their instructions to latch onto the procession of clergymen and parade down the nave in their train, where the Duke of Normandy, neo-King of England was enthroned before the altar.

The ceremony passed by Kenrick in a blur of meaningless ritual because his senses were concentrated on the structure he and his predecessors had achieved, for work had begun more than a hundred and fifty years before. Vikings had burnt down the previous building and Duke William Longespee, before his assassination, had laid the foundation stone to this much grander edifice. But all that was hearsay to Kenrick since it had happened before his birth. He had twenty-eight winters to his name and was a relative newcomer to Jumièges.

After glorying in their achievement and interpreting the construction of the building as easily as a scribe might read a psalter, his mind wandered during the long service to what he would do now that the abbey was completed. For sure, there would be more work in Normandy for a skilled mason like himself; he knew of at least three cathedrals under construction in this area alone. But his heart ached to return to Northumbria even if he had little idea of the political situation after the conquest by the ruthless Duke William. Surely, the King of England would sail back to his new realm, so why not seek passage with his numerous entourage? After this infinite consecration ceremony ended, he would ask Robert the Master Mason for advice.

He caught the mason's arm on the steps outside the west entrance,

"My friend, I wish to leave and return to my homeland but only if I can continue working as a mason."

His mentor looked at him fondly, for Kenrick had proved one of his most able protégés, showing a quickness to learn, willingness to improve and a certain ingenuity. He would be sorry to lose him but, as he could not imagine leaving his beloved Normandy, he understood Kenrick's yearning for home.

"Leave it with me, I think I know the right person to approach. Today is difficult, but on the morrow, I will put forward your name, *Saxon*."

Kenrick smiled at the swarthy-faced mason; his skin darkened by exposure to the rigours of extreme weather on towering scaffolding. He accepted the name with good grace, although not a Saxon, but an Anglian, it was no use trying to explain the difference to his companions for whom he would always be *the Saxon*.

After the ceremony, he watched the unskilled labourers piling tools and material onto ox-carts to clear the site. It was hard to believe that his years of work on this magnificent structure had come to an end. The Duke used abbeys, cathedrals and castles on a monumental scale to impress on everyone the crude power that he wielded without mercy—a reminder to his subjects that they were to obey him through the authority invested in him by the Church and thus, implicitly, God.

A voice interrupted his reverie.

"Saxon, meet me here tomorrow at noon when I hope to have news for you," said Robert de Morlaix, clapping him on the back.

The status of the master mason was such that a recommendation from him carried considerable weight. It took very little for Robert to convince King William's cleric that his Saxon mason was worthy of the most important commission the monarch might wish to bestow on him. A brief meeting with the clerk was enough to gain Kenrick passage onboard one of the ships bound for Kent. The exchange also established the mason's origins and resulted in a promise that his skills would be used in his homeland area. First, he would have to travel to London with the royal party, where his case would be dealt with and the necessary documentation provided for him. The clerk smiled thinly,

"Do not worry, friend, you will be given the post of master mason because your famed teacher has faith in you."

A few days in London and he emerged clutching a parchment with a large red wax seal, which he stowed in his saddlebag together with a purse bulging with silver coins to 'tide him over'. His instructions were to travel to Durham and present the letter to Bishop Ethelwin.

TWO

LINCOLN, LINDSEY, APRIL 1068 AD

"Hook that rope around the doorpost!"

The Norman warrior tossed the cord with an iron grapple attached to one of his men. The other end was fastened to the yoke around the shoulders of a large ox.

"You can't do this! It's my home!" A weeping woman cried. "At least let me gather some things!"

Her arms were pinned behind her back by another of the men whose task was simply to obey orders and deal with anyone, like this woman, trying to stop them executing their officers' commands.

"You should have taken your belongings when we issued the warning!"

The officer had no more time to waste on the wretched Saxon slattern. He raised his birch wand and brought it down hard on the rump of the ox, which ponderously but irresistibly thrust its weight forward, heaving the doorpost out of the ground—just like extracting a bad tooth, the Norman soldier thought. As it broke free, the front of the house collapsed, the woman writhed and spat a torrent of vile oaths, causing the officer to spin and whip the birch across her face, leaving a vicious weal, tiny prickles of blood forming across her cheek. A large stone clattered against his chain mail shirt. It had been hurled with force but when he spun around, drawing his sword, there was no sign of the offender. If he had spotted the miscreant, he'd have had him seized and then...his mind dwelt momentarily on the possible cruelties he'd have inflicted.

He knew feelings were running high here on the hilltop settlement of Lincoln. It was understandable. He and his men were invaders, conquerors, foreigners, but he didn't care about the locals' sentiments. The king had commanded the building of a castle on this strategic point and that was what they would do. It meant demolishing six hundred houses, most of them little better than hovels, nonetheless, the homes of the same number of potential enemies. Lincoln was a prosperous inland port of five thousand inhabitants. The richest among them were merchants, who traded with the lands across the North Sea, shipping wool out of ports like Boston and Lynn. They, at least were worth encouraging so that they could pay taxes into the king's coffers. The castle, once built, would enable a small garrison to keep control not just of the town but also of the surrounding area.

———

ONE MONTH LATER,

The minster church of St Mary, Lincoln

When the Normans entered the building, pushing the secular canons out of their way, Thurgot, a youth of ten and nine winters had no thoughts of resistance in mind. He was here for nothing more subversive than to learn psalmody, the art of singing psalms, something he excelled at with his fine voice and excellent pitch. This town had become his home, the centre of the bishopric of Lindsey from 678 until 958 when it became part of a huge see of Lincoln but based on Dorchester, Oxfordshire. He came from a family of landowners, of good position and had shown an aptitude for learning, making friends with some of the other Saxon youths of wealthy families.

"Which of you is named Thurgot?" the officer asked, glaring around the assembled group of curious faces. The warrior's accent was so strong that the young man understood only after repeating the words to himself twice. He did not mean to be uncooperative, but when he stepped forward, the delay earned him a painful slap across the jaw from a mailed gauntlet.

"You will come with us!"

He did not need to interpret that because the meaning was quite clear when his arms were seized by two burly soldiers and he was dragged away from his companions and outdoors to the newly constructed castle built within a month by forced labour.

It took Thurgot two days to discover why he had been taken and locked in one of the cells of the castle. That was the time needed to befriend one of the gaolers, a young man of his own race who responded shyly to Thurgot's cheerful demeanour. The captor found it strangely beguiling that the prisoner should be so buoyant in the face of his treatment and was prepared to risk the wrath of his over-seers by chancing whispered conversation. This concession made life bearable for the resilient Saxon captive and enabled him to understand his situation.

"They've taken you as a hostage. You're not the only one. It's to make sure that the most important families in the area don't organise a revolt, see?"

He did see. And he understood, but it meant that he was useful in confinement to the Normans and that might last for years and years! He couldn't have that, but how could he escape from under the noses of the well-armed and vigilant guards?

Bribery was his only hope. Knowing that a lad like his gaoler would seldom if ever have held a silver piece in his hand, he whispered,

"I have coins hidden in a pocket inside my breeches. I can give you five silver coins if you help me flee this place."

The youth's eyes widened at the suggestion. Such coins were a fortune and he believed he could arrange an escape without risk to himself.

"I need two days, my friend! Tomorrow, I'll tell you how it will be done."

The next day, he brought Thurgot a bowl of steaming chicken broth and whispered instructions.

"I will take three coins; the other two you will give to the butcher. You will pull on his son's bloodied tunic and keep the hood over your face. The guards are so dim-witted that they will not notice that he has arrived without his usual helper, but departs *with* him! When he arrives with his meat, you will be waiting, wearing the tunic I'll give you, in the kitchen to help him unload. Remember, hood up!"

That night, Thurgot could not sleep. His mind was racing, worrying about everything that could go wrong. Since he was not privy to every detail, he also worried about the unknowns that might ruin the youth's plans. Anxiously, he brooded on how they would arrive unseen in the kitchen and whether, once there, an overzealous cook might alert the guards. What he could not know was the extent of the hatred for the Norman taskmasters that meant a blind eye, deaf ears and mute tongues would be in order during his escape.

"Here, put this on! Make haste. We have a few minutes whilst the guards are changing." Thurgot shrugged himself into the white, blood-spattered over-tunic, caring little about its unsavoury smell, as long as it meant freedom from this place. Without being instructed, he pulled the hood up over his head, receiving a grunt of approval. "Come, move!" The youth locked the cell door and he followed his saviour down a blessedly empty corridor and they turned sharply into a large, smoky room where a cauldron hanging over a fire issued steam and vegetables in bunches hung from the wooden beams. The three people working there gave him only a cursory, uninterested glance, so his thumping heart calmed its racing rhythm.

They stood by the door and waited. Thurgot fumbled inside the waistband of his breeches and took out three silver coins, pressing them into his deliverer's hand.

"What will you tell them?"

"Nothing! But I'll be well away by the time they miss you. I don't want to work here, anyway!"

"Just don't get punished for helping me."

The gaoler smiled slyly,

"Shut up and remember to help the butcher unload. Just do as he says and don't forget, you owe him two silver coins. God be with you!"

His rescuer walked away without a backward glance and, alone, Thurgot at once began to worry.

What if the butcher didn't play his part?

But he needn't have troubled himself. The tradesman pushed open the door and, glancing at the bloodied white tunic, ordered,

"Untie the canvas cover then lend a hand with the swine!"

Together, they worked on the knots of the rope holding fast the flaxen sheeting and that done, hauled the covering back to expose the meat. Hoisting a heavy half side of beef onto his burly shoulder, the ceorl trudged into the kitchen, familiarly greeting the cooks. Thurgot sprang into action, glancing, without hesitation, around the courtyard to assure himself that none of the soldiers was staring at him. All appeared normal; he grasped a sectioned pig and carried it into the vast room, laying it on a table as instructed, before returning to collect the other half.

The unloading finished, the butcher said,

"Tie the canvas loosely and then hop up next to me." In a lower voice, he said, "Keep your hood up and don't say a word unless you're forced to."

The butcher urged the ox into its plodding motion and headed towards the courtyard gate. Thurgot's heart pounded in his chest, his head full of 'what ifs...?' The main one of these was...what if the guards remembered that the butcher had arrived alone? He wasn't to know that was impossible because his gaoler and the butcher had arranged arrival time to coincide with the changing of the guard. Nonetheless, to Thurgot's dismay, a rough voice ordered: "Halt!"

The guard did not as much as glance at him, but strode to the back of the cart, untied the loose knot he'd tied, raised the canvas and peered under to ensure there was no hidden fugitive. So, they were not as dim-witted as his rescuer had suggested.

"Move on!"

Never were two words more welcome. If only the ox had been as fleet-footed as a stallion! Still, the cart rolled over the wooden bridge and away into the space where once houses had stood tightly together. Thurgot bit his lip at the thought of the devastation the invaders had wrought.

"We have an agreement, lad," said the butcher.

"Ay," Thurgot nodded, fumbling for the coins inside his waistband. "Thank you for your aid, friend. I'll not forget," he said handing the coins to the eager tradesman. He made to take off the over-tunic.

"Not yet," hissed the butcher, "wait till we're well away from prying eyes."

It seemed an age before the slow-paced beast hauled them under the old Roman arch and once through it, the driver said,

"Before we reach yon houses, you take off the tunic and slip away and may God be with you!"

Without further ado, he wriggled free of the overall and laid it next to the butcher.

"Bless you, friend. Farewell!"

He glanced around to ensure no-one was observing them, noticed by only a curious goose beside a house wall, he slipped down on to the road and strode briskly away. Knowing the town like the palm of his hand was an advantage and he made directly for the old Roman road out of the settlement in direction north.

Despite the occupation of the town by the Norman conquerors, the people in the outskirts, made up of scattered houses beside the thoroughfare into the countryside, continued about their normal activities and a solitary traveller did not excite attention.

He had only to decide where to go and what to do. Clearer in his head was what *not* to do. He could not return to St Mary's church or his father's estates. The Normans were sure to search for him in both places. Unfortunately, he could think of no-one and nowhere he would be welcome or safe. As he marched jauntily downhill out of the town, stopping just once to glance back at the arrogant castle dominating the settlement, he realised that he would have to leave the country. With this in mind, he decided would head for the coast. This direction would take him towards the Humber and he remembered his father talking about a port named Grimsby. In any case, he believed it would be quieter than the busy port of Boston and, anyway, the two ports were each a little more than ten leagues from Lincoln. So, in terms of distance, there was nothing to choose between them. His mind as made up; he'd walk to Grimsby. He would be there the next morning allowing for an overnight stop. His purse still held silver coins enough to ensure a bed and a meal and more besides. He grinned and thought that God would provide for his future, the important thing was that he was free.

THREE

DURHAM, 1068 AD

The bishop's house, with its intricately carved doorposts, towered over the neighbouring buildings and Kenrick could not help admiring the trappings of worldly success conceded to a prelate. He supposed, like the abbey at Jumièges, the effort committed to impressing the Church's opulence on the populace for the glorification of the Almighty was justifiable. These musings reminded him of the situation that might undermine his schemes and those of the good bishop.

"Your Grace, there is a pressing matter that I have refrained from mentioning. All my thoughts have been on plans for the cathedral. None of them will come to fruition if we do not move to stop the rebellion."

That word stopped the prelate in his tracks as if an invisible hand had pressed against his chest.

"Rebellion, you say? Kenrick, what is it that you know?"

"I know that the king has sent a new earl to Northumbria and that he will arrive within days in Durham."

"Ay, Robert de Comines," murmured the bishop, almost

inaudibly to the mason standing beside him. In a louder voice, he asked,

"Again, I ask, what do you know?"

"I have it from a certain source that six hundred armed men are waiting for the earl's arrival, Lord Bishop, we must warn him of the danger."

"Who leads the rebels and where are they based?"

"That is the nature of the peril, Your Grace, the leaders are the most prominent noblemen in the kingdom and they wish to over-throw the foreign invader. They have thrown in their lot with the grandson of King Edmund, he who was known as the Ironside."

The face of the clergyman altered at the name of the Saxon hero and his tone became gentler,

"Ah, you refer to the aetheling." He looked thoughtful, "Mmm. Every true-blooded Saxon will be tempted to rally to Edgar. By rights, he should be our king. But where is this rebel army based? We should alert the earl to its whereabouts."

"That is difficult, as you intend it, Your Grace—"

"What do you mean?"

Taking the brusque interruption calmly, Kenrick replied,

"They are based here, in Durham, each armed man is safe within his home, ready to strike at a moment's notice. You see, the army *is* and *is not* assembled if you take my meaning. For this reason, the earl must not come to Durham."

If he comes here, I can kiss goodbye to my new cathedral.

"I agree, we must send a messenger to caution the earl not to enter the city."

Kenrick took his leave of the bishop with mixed emotions. He felt that he might have taken a step forward to save his beloved project but, at the same time, a sense of betraying his brother and his people tormented him. As he walked to his lodgings, he tried to justify his behaviour.

So, what if I have warned the Norman earl? All it means is that he won't walk into a trap in Durham. Our people can find another place

to fight and I'll be free to build a monument to the glory of God. How can that be wrong?

However much he tried to set his nagging conscience to rest, deep down he knew he had deprived the Saxons of their best chance of surprising the foe. But in this, he was mistaken, too.

―――――

ONE DAY LATER, *ten leagues north of York.*

The cleric dismounted and was at once escorted to the earl.

"Lord, I bear an important message from the Bishop of Durham," the young clergyman looked with disapproval at the arrogant features of the dark-haired foreigner, so different in appearance from the Anglian lords he was used to seeing around the bishop's house.

Unceremoniously, the Norman earl snatched the proffered parchment, studied the crest of the wax seal, broke it open and swiftly read the note before screwing it contemptuously in his hand and flinging it to the ground.

"Tell your Lord Bishop that I will bring my men to Durham as commanded by the king."

"But, my Lord—"

The proud countenance contorted and Robert de Comines, unaccustomed to being gainsaid, spat,

"Begone!" adding in a hiss, "Before I have you whipped for disobedience."

The cleric retreated hastily, bowing as he stepped backwards,

"As you command, Lord!"

He heard the scornful aside as he turned to depart,

"Saxon curs! Unfit even to act as messengers."

I'm glad you ignored the warning. I hope you get your come-uppance.

The sentiment of the messenger might as well have been a *pre-*sentiment. The Norman rode up the hill into Durham in his chain mail shirt, at the head of a sizeable force. After receiving the bishop's admonition, he was alert to danger but did not expect it to come from the seemingly quiet houses lining the road winding uphill. Suddenly, without warning, men with axes rushed from the humble buildings and, taking full advantage of surprise, wreaked devastating damage on the column of Norman soldiers, well-armed and -armoured as they were. The victory was secured before the unprepared newcomers to the town could regroup. At the head of his men, the earl shouted orders in vain and realising his plight, rallied the small group immediately at his back,

"Come, follow me! We will take shelter."

With no more than a dozen men, he rode to the bishop's house, dismounted, evaded the contents of a pail full of boiling water flung from one of the houses opposite and glared in disbelief at the steam rising from the ground where the water had landed. He would deal with that slut later! He hammered on the door, and gained admittance, only to learn that Bishop Ethelwin was not expecting him and was not in residence. His futile rage did not spare the servants, whom he organised with oaths and kicks to move heavy furniture against the front and back doors. Realising that with only a dozen soldiers, he was heavily outnumbered, he regretted the short shrift he had given to the bishop's messenger. Evidently, the prelate had believed the warning would suffice and had not expected his arrival in the town. Unless the bishop was colluding with the Saxons...not an impossibility, wasn't Ethelwin a Saxon, himself? When he established his authority over this wretched land, he would rule with an iron fist and all the key positions would be entrusted to reliable men of Norman stock. These were his thoughts as, spirit quailing, he heard futile battering on the outside of the door that gave onto the road.

A veteran of Hastings and previous battles won by Duke— or as he as now, King— William, Robert de Comines was no coward but he trembled at the fury outside the building. What he could not foresee was that danger would come from within, but not from the Saxon servants but fire. He had not thought to barricade the windows, contenting himself with positioning his soldiers there in case some reckless assailant should attempt to clamber in. He had not imagined that they would hurl burning brands into the house and when the realisation came, it was too late to stop the flames from flaring up the drapes and catching hold of the wooden furniture not piled against the doors.

The small amount of water the servants were able to provide in reaction to the danger was ineffectual and with his sword, he slew a maid he caught flinging cooking oil onto a woollen wall-hanging, little realising that in his rage, he had consigned her to a more merciful death. Soon, the room was full of smoke and the flames were beginning to leap taller than a man. The earl pushed one of his men out of his way as he tried to flee into the rear of the building. He slipped on the oil the treacherous girl had spilt and the weight of his mail shirt made it difficult for him to rise but, in any case, there was more air, less smoke, near the floor and he began to crawl, drawing greedy breaths, into the kitchen area. His ears rang with the screams of men and women succumbing to the flames in the front room, but as he crawled and scrambled into the rear of the bishop's home, he knew he, too, was doomed.

His narrowed eyes, peering through the choking billowing smoke watched helplessly as he saw more firebrands arcing into the room through the kitchen window. Even if he succeeded in reaching the blessed air of the aperture, how could he escape? He had given the order to pile the furniture against the door and even if he reached the casement, surely an axe would be there to bite deep into his flesh. How he cursed the day William the Bastard had sent him to the north into this God-forsaken land. What had made him leave his beloved Normandy?

The heat was atrocious and as the flames drew nearer amid the choking fumes, his metal armour heated beyond endurance. He was being cooked alive in the very mail that was supposed to protect him. Coughing and spluttering, Robert began to wrestle and grope with the shirt in a feeble attempt to shed it from his body. The more he struggled, the more he was condemned to breathe in the toxic fumes and before long, he collapsed prone and unconscious, blessedly unaware of the flames that would soon consume his body.

Bishop Ethelwin, less than a mile from his home gazed at the black smoke rising in a pall over the hilltop. Something was amiss, he knew, alertedby the raised voices that could be heard even from that distance.

"Kenrick. We should go and see what is happening. There is a great fire in the town. Hark! Do you hear screaming? Come! Our calculations can wait for another time.

Can it be that the Normans have come and are slaughtering the people?

These were Kenrick's completely mistaken thoughts, as they hurried towards the bishop's home. The first realisation of how wrong had been his assumption came when they saw the first bloodied bodies of the mailed Norman soldiers lying, as they had died, in a column along the thoroughfare. The great number of slain Normans told a different tale. There was no sign of the inhabitants, for had he and the bishop known, they were screaming and gesticulating their hatred outside the inferno that had been the bishop's residence.

The prelate grasped Kenrick's arm, his eyes were wild,

"That's my house!" he cried, "Gone! With all my belongings."

"Your Grace, thank the Lord you were not inside," Kenrick tried to offer comfort. Even as he spoke, he spotted his brother, his axe hanging limply by his side, shouting to people to stand clear of the flaming building, for sparks were flying and blazing wooden beams crashing dangerously to ground. Kenrick heard him call for water to stop the flames spreading to the adjoining buildings. Some people, presumably the owners themselves had already begun this work.

"Fetch buckets! Get water," Edwy cried, gesticulating and pushing men with his free hand. "We must save what we can! Our work is done here!"

"Who is that man?" Bishop Ethelwin asked Kenrick.

"Surely, you know him, Your Grace? Is it that his face is blackened with smoke? That is Ealdorman Edwy…my brother."

"Can it be that your brother has led this revolt and destroyed my home? There will be consequences. The king's ire will be terrible."

"That's why I tried to warn you, Your Grace."

"Ay, in truth, you did. So, these invaders can be defeated." Kenrick gazed in surprise at the prelate. There was no doubt that despite the loss of his possessions, there was enthusiasm in his tone. Did the bishop, after all, sympathise with the rebels? He was soon to find out because the clergyman pushed his way to stand beside the ealdorman.

"That was my home you've burnt down."

"Ah, Bishop! Thank God you are safe! I feared you were in there with the Norman swine!"

"Praise the Lord, I was in the company of your brother."

"Ah, Kenrick! You did well to keep the bishop safe."

Kenrick smiled but he wasn't going to admit otherwise within the hearing of the triumphant mob.

"There will be reprisals," the cleric said earnestly.

"Which is why we must move before William the Bastard does. Aetheling Edgar and a Danish army await our forces. We'll march on York."

Kenrick gaped at the bishop when he said,

"And I will ride with you. I can wield weapons in a righteous cause, my son. I will bless our men before the battle, too."

There's no way the damned cathedral will be built now!

Kenrick's high hopes of the morning when he had discussed quantities of stone with the bishop, were nought but ashes now, like the prelate's home. He trudged back unhappily to his lodgings, wondering vaguely whether he should join his brother and the clergyman in the proposed attack on York.

He considered what kind of person he was. A warrior? Not in spirit—the bishop was more warlike than he—but he knew that his family vaunted a strong tradition of combatants, men who had contributed to the creation of the great Northumbria of the past. What was so wrong with wanting to be creative? Some of his forebears managed that, too. He thought of the famous Aella, the leather-worker and scribe, then there was Cynn, true not an artist, but he had created a new breed of horse. And hadn't he, Kenrick, learnt how to cut and dress squared stones, not to mention the exquisite angel he'd carved for the abbey at Jumièges? Was wanting to dedicate his life to his craft so wrong, no matter who the ruler?

FOUR

COUENEBI, LINDSEY, APRIL 1068 AD

THE ADVANTAGE OF MARCHING ON A ROMAN ROAD, AS THURGOT discovered, is that there are no surprises around the bend. The Ermine Street lay straight as a reed and he strode along seeing few people about their agricultural tasks near the sparse settlements. The weather stayed fair and only one brief shower had him sheltering under a tree but the weak sun managed to cheer the wet landscape after the short interlude. In this way, he covered the leagues without much fatigue also because the route contained few hills. Towards evening, he came to a hamlet called Couenebi, which was the ideal place for an overnight stop. Firstly, the settlement was where he would have to leave the Roman road, otherwise, it would take him north to the Humber estuary to a place where the Romans legionaries could wade across on those rare occasions when the weather and the tides combined to make it possible. Not that Thurgot appreciated that; all he knew was that he had to strike east if he wanted to reach the coast at Grimsby. The road forked and to his satisfaction, there stood a tavern, where he was able to obtain a room for the night. The innkeeper told him the snippet about the estuary crossing. He added that the Ermine Street also split, striking off to the north-west so that the ancient invaders could march around the Humber to continue northwards in adverse conditions.

To further enhance his good mood, the ale was to his liking and there was the promise of music because a travelling scop had chosen, like him, to stay for the night. The minstrel was strumming his hearpe distractedly for the moment, but towards the end of Thurgot's meal, he began a traditional local saga about the founding of Grimsby. The rich alliterative language and the pleasant timbre of the scop's voice enthralled the tired traveller, who soon picked up the refrain and joined in with his splendid voice. This earned him encouraging smiles from the singer and the innkeeper alike. Thurgot regretted that he did not know the words of the saga, but on the other hand, it was a pleasant surprise to hear the legend of the heroic Havelock the Dane unfold.

When he finally retired for the night and lay on his bed, the tale filled his mind so that he did not worry about what the morrow would bring. Hearing the story of Grim the fisherman had given him a taste to discover the next day the coastal settlement founded by the wanderer of the saga.

He tried to recall the words of the scop as he lay there. How did the poem begin? In the reign of Athelwold, a just and virtuous king, who dies without a male heir and leaves his young daughter Goldborow to the care of Godrich, Earl of Cornwall, who is to rule as regent until Goldborow can be married. Athelwold insisted that she should be wed to the *highest man in England*. After Athelwold's death, Godrich immediately betrays his oath and imprisons Goldborow in a remote tower in Dover. Thurgot grunted: just like he'd been held in Lincoln.

He bit his lower lip and tossed and turned in bed, trying to recall the next verse. At last, it came to him, and in the silence of his room, he began to quietly hum the refrain. Sleep eluded him. Was it the excitement of his escape from the castle that still had him on edge? He remembered that the saga shifted to Denmark. Wasn't there another traitor? Ay, across the sea in Denmark another virtuous king,

Birkabein, dies, leaving behind two daughters— he could not remember their names— and a son, Havelock. Godard, a wealthy retainer, is appointed regent. Godard too betrays his trust: he brutally murders the daughters by cutting their throats and hands the three-year-old Havelock over to a thrall, the fisherman Grim, to be drowned in the sea. Grim recognizes Havelock as the rightful heir to the kingdom when he sees a pair of miraculous signs: a bright light that emerges from the boy's mouth when he is sleeping, and a cross-shaped birthmark on his shoulder. Grim is persuaded to spare Havelock's life but tells Godard that he has killed the child.

Thurgot yawned but shook off sleep—reconstructing the saga had become a challenge for him— Grim flees with his family and Havelock to England, where he founds the town of Grimsby at the estuary of the Humber. Thurgot would see the port for himself the next day. Havelock is brought up as part of Grim's family and works as a fisherman alongside Grim and his sons. And here was the chorus that he had joined in with. The exact words came to him and keeping his voice to a whisper so as not to disturb anyone, he repeated them. The scop had been superb and Thurgot, who considered he had a better singing voice, imagined himself as a wandering minstrel but knew in his heart that he loved psalmody. He could not imagine abandoning his years of training to use his voice, other than in the service of God —that would be a waste.

Refrain over, he returned to piecing together the saga. Havelock grows to extraordinary size and strength, and has a huge appetite; during a time of famine, Grim is unable to feed him, and Havelock leaves home to seek his subsistence in Lincoln, barefoot and clad in a cloak made from an old sail. So, just like himself, the hero had a hard time in the same city. Strangely, Thurgot was drawing comfort from this tale. He realised that it was giving him the courage to face his adventure beginning the next day.

In Lincoln, Havelock is taken in by Bertram, a cook in a noble household, and works for him as a kitchen-boy. Havelock's humility, gentleness and cheerful nature make him popular and his unusual height, strength and beauty draw attention wherever he goes. In a stone-throwing competition he is far better than the other young men with his near-superhuman might. This victory makes him briefly the wonder of the day and brings him to the notice of Godrich, who is present in Lincoln for a parliament. Godrich notices Havelock's unusual height and decides to arrange a marriage between him and Goldborow, as this will, in a cunning way, fulfil the terms of his promise to Athelwold that Goldborow should marry the *highest* man in the kingdom. Believing Havelock to be a peasant's son, he intends to cheat Goldborow out of her inheritance by the marriage.

Thurgot growled under the blanket, wasn't his luck similar to the maid's, he being deprived of his inheritance by the actions of ruthless invaders? But hadn't the scop sung of a happy outcome? Why should there not be one for him?

In the saga, Havelock is reluctant to wed because he is too poor to support a wife, but submits after being threatened by Godrich. Havelock and Goldborow marry and return to Grimsby, where they are taken in by Grim's children. That night Goldborow is awakened by a bright light and sees a flame coming out of Havelock's mouth. She then notices his birthmark, and an angel-voice tells her of Havelock's royal lineage and his destiny to become king of Denmark and England. When they wake, she shares her vision and they agree to return to Denmark.

Thurgot hummed the refrain again and although he wasn't sleeping, he was feeling optimistic and cheerful. And now he had come to the part he'd enjoyed best—the triumphant conclusion. Havelock sails to Denmark with Goldborow to reclaim his kingdom. A Danish nobleman, Ubbe, recognises Havelock as the son of Birkabein and immediately pledges his support to Havelock in overthrowing Godard.

Thurgot grinned to himself under his blanket and decided that he too, one day, would triumph. When Havelock receives the submission of many of the Danish lords, he defeats Godard and the usurper is condemned to be flayed and hanged. Havelock invades England, overthrows Godrich in battle and claims the throne in Goldborow's name. As king of Denmark and England, Havelock rules justly for more than sixty years. He and Goldborow enjoy a happy, loving marriage, and have many children: all their sons become kings and all their daughters, queens.

And all this began in Grimsby as does my adventure in the morning.

With this comforting thought, Thurgot slipped into a deep, refreshing sleep. Still in a cheerful mood the next morning, he set off on the last stage of his journey and passing marshland, arrived in the River Freshney basin where Grim had supposedly founded the settlement and where many vessels were tied up. Some were fishing boats but he was more interested in the larger trading ships.

Circumstances favoured his plans as King William wished to promote friendly relations with Norway. The king knew that Norway had lost most of its nobility at the Battle of Stamford Bridge in 1066. He sent envoys charged to go to Norway and these Normans were due to sail from Grimsby. Thurgot, whose mother was Norwegian and father Saxon, had grown up speaking the language, hence also his Norse name, dedicated to the god Thor although he was brought up Christian. His knowledge of Norwegian meant he could eavesdrop on what the crew was saying; therefore, he realised that this was the ship for him— if he wished to start a new life where better than in a country where he knew the language? So, by careful spying and timing, he stowed away unseen. Silent and still, he remained hidden until the motion of the sea told him that they had cast off. Nonetheless, he decided that it was wiser to remain concealed under the canvas cover he had found until the ship was well away from the shore. Unfortunately, a sailor about his work pulled away the sheet hiding him and let out an understandable cry of surprise.

Thurgot leapt to his feet but two other Norse sailors grabbed him and held him until the captain came to find out what the commotion was about. The Norman envoys also came one with his sword aggressively in hand.

"A stowaway!" he cried accusation in his tone. "He's probably a fugitive from justice. Captain, you must turn back and deliver him to the authorities."

The captain looked up at his sail and beyond to the clear sky. They were already making excellent progress and he did not wish to return.

Thurgot took advantage of his hesitation, speaking in Norwegian fluently and confidently.

"Captain, I am not a fugitive. My name is Thurgot and my mother is from your country. I am happy to work my passage. I should have sought your permission but I knew these louts would not want me aboard. That's why I hid."

The captain looked anxiously at the Normans but their ignoring Thurgot's insult told him they could not understand. He turned to face the man with the drawn sword,

"Put your weapon away. This man is no criminal, he is a distant relative of mine. He played a joke to surprise me! See how it worked. Ha-ha! There's no need to return to the port."

Thurgot nodded and grinned at the Normans. Still glaring with suspicion in his eyes, nonetheless, the man sheathed his sword and the stowaway thanked his knowledge of the language, for it was that which convinced the envoys that the captain was telling the truth. The mariner threw his arm around Thurgot's shoulder and drew him away from the passengers.

"Come, I'd better set you to work or they might prove difficult. See that rope, it's untidy. Coil it neatly, that should convince them. When you've done that, join me in the stern at the steer board and you can tell me what you're up to."

Coiling rope is not hard and his effort was tidy enough. All the while, he was conscious of the Norman eyes on him, so he was happy to make his way to the captain and leave them amidships.

The seafarer explained to Thurgot that they would put into a

Danish port before sailing on to Norway. He had wool, hides and lambskins to trade for casks of salted herring. But his cargo of porpoise meat and wine from Rouen would go directly to Nidaros in Norway.

"If you are wise and able, my friend, you will come to prominence in Nidaros, for they say that King Olav III is open to foreigners at his court."

Thurgot was receptive to this idea and whilst he was tempted by the wealth on display to remain in the bustling port of Heidaby in Denmark, his command of Norwegian persuaded him to stick to his original plan. This proved to be a fortunate decision.

At Nidaros, he made his way to the new cathedral. It was a small stone church built on the site of the grave of the martyred Saint Olav. Inside the edifice, he attended a psalm session but was disappointed to hear the psalms recited. When the service ended, he waited and approached the priest, upbraiding him for not having sung the psalms.

"You know, don't you that they were written with the purpose of being sung?"

"Well, young man, we have no expertise in psalmody. I agree with you that the language is beautiful and lends itself to music."

"Father, the word *psalm* in Hebrew refers to a musical instrument, so I think there's no debate to be had on the matter."

"Have you studied psalmody, my son?"

"Ay, Father, in Lincoln. I am a Saxon cleric, but I speak your language since my mother was born near Trondheim. Would you like to hear a psalm?"

From memory and in Latin, Thurgot tilted back his head, took a deep breath and intoned a psalm in his rich, cultured voice. The priest looked at him in amazement and listened raptly until the end."

"Quite enthralling, my friend. Psalm 91, was it not? *Deus meus, in quem sperabo—*

My God in whom I will trust."

"Ah, I wonder whether you would be interested in teaching

psalmody to the brothers? I could make an official request to the king. What say you? Could you teach them in our tongue?"

"Well, ay, if you have the texts."

He was excited. He could not have hoped for a better start in Norway; or had God contrived this opportunity for him?

FIVE

YORK, NORTHUMBRIA, 1069 AD

Bishop Ethelwin, stirred by victory over a Norman earl and seven hundred men, decided that the time was right to fulfil the will of the English people, who had acclaimed the young Aetheling Edgar king in London on the death of Harold in 1066. After contacting the seventeen-year-old prince, he gathered an army and marched on York, strengthened by the imminent arrival of a promised three hundred Danish longships heading for the Humber estuary. The moment could hardly have been better. There was trouble on the Welsh border, where a rebellious thegn named Eadric had joined forces with the Welsh kings and the men of Chester. In the south-west, the men of Devon and Cornwall were in revolt. Also, across the Channel, William had lost Maine.

Edwy went to his brother's lodgings and seized him by the arm.

"See what we achieved in Durham. There's no turning back! We must shake off Norman rule whilst they are reeling. We need every strong man for the attack on York. When Northumbria is in Saxon hands, you can build as many cathedrals as you like!"

"It takes more than a man's lifetime to construct *one* cathedral,

Edwy. But, ay, I will come with you. We must struggle to hold onto our family estates."

He did not want to fight but he had seen Norman intentions in Durham and, although they had suffered defeat, their arrogant will to dominate and place their people in key positions might well deprive him of what he wanted most—to become a master mason. Bishop Ethelwin had spoken of grandiose plans for Durham, so why not throw in his lot with the prelate? These thoughts he kept to himself, displaying only the patriotic fervour his brother wished to see.

The ease of taking York was an illusion. The rebels had high hopes of defeating King William, but the Norman ruler, used to a life of political survival, sent envoys to the Danes and by paying vast sums of money, persuaded them to leave England in the spring. Scouts came hurrying to Bishop Ethelwin and Edgar Aetheling each day with ever more disheartening news. William had left the problem of the south-western insurrection to his deputies, first confronting the Welsh and their allies, crushing them at Stafford, before marching northeast to Nottingham. As Christ's Mass approached, the king began to march towards York, confident that he had the strength to crush the rebellion.

Edwy's words to Kenrick underlined the dire situation.

"There's nought for it, brother, we must flee. The Norman bastard is too strong for us. Although we could hold out for months in this city, defeat or starvation are not choices I would gladly face. If we return home and do not raise arms against the invaders, there is a chance they will leave us in peace."

"The King will have vengeance for what happened in Durham," unconvinced, Kenrick shook his head, "But you're right, staying here can only lead to disaster."

They were not the only ones to reason in this way and the aetheling was among the first to flee the city. Bishop Ethelwin, spoke with his noble supporters.

"All is lost, my friends, William descends upon us and will be here in two days. We do not have the strength to face him after the

Danes abandoned us to the wolves. We must throw ourselves on his mercy."

The turncoat Earl of Northumbria, Gospatric, now spoke,

"The Bishop is right but I suggest you do not rely on William's clemency but follow my lead. I mean to defend Bamburgh with all my men. Not even William will risk an attack on that fortress."

"In that case, I'll cross to Lindisfarne and take what Church treasures I can save to the Holy Isle," the prelate said.

Others discussed their plans openly so that by nightfall, not one of the lords remained in York. This did nothing to assuage William's fury. Disappointed not to fight a pitched battle and settle scores once and for all with the rebellious north, he consulted with his councillors and decided on a severe plan to deal with Northumbria.

Many of the rebels had taken to hiding in the hills and woodlands, so William spent Christ's Mass in the city before beginning a campaign of what he glibly called *harrowing*—that is, weeding out and eliminating the Northumbrian renegades. By destroying the region's resources thoroughly, he sought to put an end to the cycle of rebellions by ensuring that any future insurgents would lack the means to support themselves. The campaign was as efficient as it was effective. William's armies spread out over more than one hundred miles of territory, as far north as the River Tyne. In the course of just a few weeks, he demonstrated the punishment that awaited those who rose against him and also snuffed out what lingering hopes the rebels might have had of driving out the invaders.

At Cowesby, Kenrick and Edwy first knew about this when screaming came from the village and a ceorl burst into the farmyard, pointing at the smoke rising from burning barns and houses beyond the palisade.

"Lord, make good your escape! The Normans are upon us! They are slaughtering everyone—even the bairns! There are many of them, you cannot hold the farm, Lord! Flee!"

Edwy began to protest that he was an ealdorman and that the

Normans could not do this to him, but Kenrick grabbed his arm and shook him,

"Don't be a fool! I told you this would happen! We must take horses and bolt to the moors. They will not follow us into the wilds."

He was right, but there remained the problem of food. There was no time to take foodstuffs and if they wished to make good their escape, a lumbering ox-cart laden with provisions would ruin their chances. There was just time to gather the horses and as many men as they could convince before the first pillagers burst into the courtyard. None of the fugitives stopped to watch the destruction of their home-stead. Much as they disliked the thought, ahead of them now stretched the life of an outlaw. At least, they were alive. Whether Edwy would regain the status of ealdorman was a thought that paled into insignificance compared to worrying where their next meal would come from. Several of the band of ten men had had the pres-ence of mind to gather up a bow and a quiver full of arrows. The moorland provided them with some game, especially fowl, for finding deer was an almost impossible task, at least, so it proved at first until they learnt the hunting skills required to stalk and bring down a stag.

William had begun harrying the north in the winter, which made survival more difficult. The horses were the lifeline for Edwy and his small band. Their occasional visits down from the moors showed them how horrendous the plight of the Northumbrians had become. No village remained inhabited between York and Durham and the countryside lay empty and uncultivated. They did not know it but this situation would continue for years. The few people they encoun-tered, living in hiding, told terrible tales of others reduced to eating donkeys, cats and dogs. Kenrick felt like killing one man who confessed to having eaten human flesh in desperation.

They made a home in a crag, where a cavern provided shelter for men and horses when the weather turned hostile. It did this frequently and rapidly on the moors but they learnt to recognise the signs of change in the air and avoided exposing themselves more than necessary to adverse conditions. They would have liked to construct stables around the cavemouth but as Kenrick, the most practical among them, pointed out, building would betray their presence to anyone searching for fugitives. The additional comfort would not be worth the price of their lives. Their forays out of the moors revealed that the Normans continued to hunt down their enemies and William made no effort to control his fury, punishing the innocent with the guilty. He ordered that crops, herds, tools and food be burned to ashes; countless people perished of starvation.

Kenrick gave serious thought to his situation. He was not prepared to live as an outlaw forever. If he could not achieve his dream of becoming a master mason in England, he would take a ship and join one of the great construction sites in Normandy. He could speak the language and had the skills to be instantly employed. He would be happy to be a simple mason and work under another master. Only, it would sadden him to leave Edwy and the others, for they had built a strong friendship over the winter, sharing hardships. He decided he would seek out Bishop Ethelwin on Lindisfarne first, for if there was any hope of resuming their scheme, he would seize it with both hands. Even to his optimistic mind, the chances of this happening seemed remote; nonetheless, he would attempt the visit as soon as he reassured himself of his friends' wellbeing.

As it happened, having effectively subdued the population, William carried out a complete replacement of Anglo-Saxon leaders with Norman ones in the North. The new aristocracy in England was predominantly of Norman extraction; however, one exception was that of Alan Rufus, a trusted Breton lord, who in 1069–1071 obtained a substantial fiefdom north of York, which the Normans called *the Hundred of the Land of Count Alan*. Thanks to this nobleman a new prospect opened for Edwy. Alan, governed his own 'principality' and excluded other Norman lords, implementing a policy of retaining the surviving Anglo-Danish lords or their heirs. Since Edwy was one of these, Alan sent a messenger to find the ealdorman and confirmed that the fugitive was no longer an outlaw but could return to reconstruct his lands and make them once again productive. The condition being that he would swear allegiance to Count Alan and, in consequence to King William.

At first, Edwy was doubtful but Kenrick said,

"You would be mad not to accept. This is the chance to keep the family estates. It will be hard to build up from nothing again, but you have men to toil in the fields and horses. I will stay for some months to oversee building work. We can construct barns and homes now that the fair weather is setting in. I will only leave you when you are re-established. Go, swear your allegiance to this count, all you have to lose is your pride—and that, as you know, brother, is a sin."

Edwy, unable to resist the lure of maintaining lands that had been in the family for generations, bent the knee and to his satisfaction, despite his diffidence, discovered that he liked the Breton.

"Bretons are different from Normans," he told all his companions. If we fulfil our obligations, Alan will leave us in peace. We clasped hands on it."

Kenrick did not share his brother's confidence, but then, he hadn't met the man as Edwy had. What seemed clear to him was the good sense of the count's scheme. In this way, he assured himself of the goodwill of the landowners and their loyalty. Nobody in his right mind would want to return to a life of deprivation. Edwy's land had proved bountiful over the centuries and with the necessary effort, there was no reason why it should not be so once more.

As a result of the depopulation, their Breton overlord sought settlers to work in the fields. Edwy was more than willing to rent lands to any men not openly disloyal to his new master. He came to accept that the rebellion had failed and was a thing of the past. Unlike the Vikings in the centuries before, the Normans did not settle wholesale in Northumbria, but only occupied the upper ranks of society. This allowed Edwy and Kenrick's Anglo-Scandinavian culture to survive beneath Norman rule and everyone was reasonably contented.

The farmstead at Cowesby returned to its former situation. Many of the nearby dependent villages never recovered but one or two, like

Flasby, were settled again by eager Danes, thus, although the brothers did not know it, history repeated itself exactly. The clear brook running through the woodland and the fertile soil made it the ideal place for settlers once again.

Seeing the preconditions for prosperity in place, Kenrick bade sorrowful farewell to his brother and comrades and in the late summer of 1070 rode to Bamburgh with the idea of crossing to Lindisfarne and seeking out Bishop Ethelwin. In a tavern in the town, he discovered that the bishop had tried to flee with many Northumbrian treasures—including the body of Saint Cuthbert to Lindisfarne but he was caught, outlawed, imprisoned, and now suffering ill-health, was unable to speak with visitors. Therefore, Kenrick, still nurturing his dream, decided to remain in Bamburgh and seek to enter the Earl's good graces. From his possession of Bamburgh castle, Earl Gospatric was able to make terms with King William, who left him undisturbed. But his situation was precarious and Kenrick, who had trouble gaining close access to the earl, learnt from others that far from fostering grandiose schemes, Gospatric was forced to pay heavy taxes to the vindictive King, who only tolerated his continued presence and rank on suffrage. Several of his new acquaintances warned Kenrick to keep his distance and to await better times.

Luckily, he followed this advice, more out of circumstances than through a definite plan of his own. As it happened, his enforced procrastination would lead in time to exceptional circumstances allowing him to fulfil his dreams. Momentarily, he wasted his talents working as a simple building labourer. His willingness, strength and expertise ensured there was always coin in his purse and he lived well enough in Bamburgh for almost two years before events turned in his favour.

SIX

NORTHUMBRIA, LATE MARCH 1074

THE WEATHER WORSENED TO A FULL GALE, HEAVY RAIN LASHED the decks of the Norwegian ship and Thurgot's attempts to shelter under the gunwales proved futile. His sopping cloak hung heavily and, instead of offering protection against the wind and rain, made him feel more wretched. There came a change in wind direction to due North. At this, the steersman was aided to run before the wind and seek shelter behind the Farne Islands. Except that, despite Thurgot's prayers for salvation, the vessel struck aground with considerable force, on Longstone, one of the Outer Farne Islands. The ship broke her back and filled rapidly with water. Men, thrown off their feet, cried in panic and some scrambled over the wooden wall of the ship's side to jump clear of the doomed wreck so as not to be sucked under.

Thurgot stared in horror at the angry gigantic waves crashing deafeningly against the fanged rocks. A body hurled onto one of those jagged crags would have no hope of survival. He thought frantically—his heavy, wet clothing would drag him beneath the surface. Not a strong swimmer, he needed something to cling to. His first thought was his treasure chest but he doubted its buoyancy—better to stay alive than to drown for his fortune. Shedding his cumbersome cloak, he seized an oar and threw himself overboard on the seaward side of the craft. At once, he was flung against the wooden hull, knocking the breath out of him but luckily, he remained conscious and still clinging to the unwieldy pole. Using his feet, he pushed backwards but the next great wave dashed him against the hull once more, this time, he lost consciousness momentarily. When he revived, he was clear of the ill-starred vessel, although he could see nothing thanks to the raging sea. His arm draped over the solid oar felt as if it might be torn off. He tried to adjust himself but feared to lose his grip if he struggled too much on the slippery wood: his one hope of survival. The numbness in his arm was the main risk of disaster but Thurgot could not imagine how quickly the furious waves were thrusting him towards safety.

Five miles from the wreck, he was raised and dropped in endless vertiginous surges, but the sea was running so fast that within the hour, still unknown to him, he was only hundreds of yards from a beach. The coast to the south of Lindisfarne was fringed with sandy beaches and, ashore, Kenrick, whose master had sent him away for the day from their outdoor site because the foul weather made construction impractical, had decided to ride there to gaze upon the agitated sea and breathe in the bracing air. It was folly in the teeming rain, but Kenrick loved the majesty of Nature in all her moods and he had nothing else to do.

He gazed out over the water, impressed by the serried rushing rollers breaking on the shore, flinging foam high into the air. Peering, eyes almost closed to thwart the rain, for an instant he glimpsed a dark shape on the crest of a wave. A seal, maybe? There it was again! But this time, Kenrick saw the long wooden oar. Surely it was some poor mariner hanging onto an oar—he must save him! He unfastened his cloak and laid it over the back of his horse, considered stripping off his tunic but, shivering in the cold March air, he decided to try to reach the castaway in what clothes he had on. A sturdy man, Kenrick was a strong swimmer but defying such tempestuous waves tested him to the full. He timed his entry as best he could but had to use much energy to make headway to where he thought he had seen the unfortunate sailor. Flayed by the waves, he shook his head to clear his vision when he decided to tread water and raised high, in a fleeting instant, he glimpsed what he sought some thirty yards ahead. Striking out with all his might, he cleverly pushed arms straight into each towering wave, so that he wasn't swept backwards. In this way, he reached the man draped over the wooden pole. The poor fellow was pale and seemed more dead than alive—and in no condition to help himself. Kenrick pulled him by his clothing free of the oar. It would be easier to make the shore without it. Placing a strong builder's arm under the castaway's armpit and around his back, Kenrick, with the sea to aid him, swam with his other hand and kicked frantically with his feet, relieved to find he was making rapid progress. Amid the mighty waves, he had no idea how far they were from the beach, but he did know that they were being swept along at considerable speed. Suddenly, he heard the crash of breakers and smiled despite his suffering because his supporting arm was on fire from holding his human flotsam's head above water. At this point, he did not know whether his efforts were in vain. Was the man living or not? Still, he had to try—what if their situations had been reversed? Wouldn't he have wanted his rescuer to make every effort to save him? The sound of the breakers grew louder, he waited and judging the motion of the giant waves, when he was in a trough, let his feet find the sea bed. There it was! But useless! The next wave flung him off his feet and forward, head underwater. This happened again and again until Kenrick could no longer swim and had to hope that the sea would be merciful because the waves tossed them like defenceless babes. He twisted a knee attempting to gain his footing but managed to drag and heave his limp companion onto the beach.

They had both swallowed too much seawater trying to get free of the waves, but the castaway looked in a much worse state. Kenrick bent over him and pressed down on the man's chest. After pumping for several moments, the fellow gasped, a gush of water issuing from his mouth. Then, he battled for breath and Kenrick hoisted him to a sitting position. This had the effect of sending more water spouting from the sailor's mouth, causing him to cough and splutter, but, to Kenrick's relief, he began breathing freely.

As if waking from a nightmare, the mason limped to his horse and seized his cloak. Wet through and shivering, he wanted nothing more than to wrap it around himself. Instead, he reached down and the man he'd rescued clasped his hand. Kenrick hauled him to his feet and flung the mantle around his shoulders. Without it, the mariner would probably die of exposure.

"Come," he said, voice made gruff by the salt in his mouth, "Up you get or you'll catch your death of cold."

He helped the man into the saddle and asked, "Can you ride?"

"Ay," nothing more was added to the feeble reply.

He considered mounting the horse behind the other but dismissed the idea partly for the sake of the poor dappled grey mare, for he was a big man and, also because he needed to get warm, so ignoring the ache in his knee, he began to run towards Bamburgh, his horse trotting dutifully behind him. He soon began to feel life returning to his chilled limbs, too much, because a stitch in his side demanded he slowed down. Luckily, he had ridden to the nearest stretch of beach from the town and before his strength failed him, the walls rose above them. He took the reins and walked ahead of his mount, assuring himself that his merman was alive.

Well known to the guards, he passed through the gate with a cursory,

"Saved him from a shipwreck. He needs warmth."

"Give him some scalding broth," said the tall guard with a grin.

Kenrick took the horse to his lodgings, left it with a stable lad, made the promise of a coin later and helped his companion up the stairs to his room. He revived the night's embers into cheerful flames and carried over an iron tripod to hang a bowl of the same material from over the fire. Soon a hot broth would restore them both. It was the guard's suggestion, but also the easiest food to prepare as well as what they needed. He chopped vegetables and threw them into the small cauldron followed by a handful of dried beans.

An anxious glance at his visitor, steam rising from his cloak, reassured him that despite his shivering, he was better. This, he could see from the colour returning to his cheeks and the alert eyes that were following his every action.

"Another few minutes and the beans will be ready."

"I owe you my life. I'd never have cheated the sea on my own. What is your name? Who do I have to thank?"

"Thank God, friend. But my name is Kenrick. I am a mason, or at least, I *was* a mason."

The guest looked sharply at the bitterness in his tone and decided to understand better later. First, he must explain something.

"Kenrick. I am a Saxon but have come from Norway. Unfortunately, the weather betrayed us. It seemed set fair when we sailed, but then suddenly..." he trailed off hopelessly.

"The sea is like that. The sea and the mountains both. One minute you're happily enjoying good weather and then—"

"Ay, that's how it was. I dare say I'm the only one left alive. I've lost everything, too. I was coming with a chest of coins and now the crabs are spending my silver!"

He looked miserable as the thought that he was destitute struck him.

"Friend, I cannot pay you for your kindness. Not yet, at least."

"I seek no payment. Only a name."

"Oh ay, forgive me. It's Thurgot and my family lives in Lindsey if they're still alive."

"I thought you said you were a Saxon?"

"I did. Ah, my name? My mother is Norwegian but my father is Saxon and I grew up in Lincoln. Where are we exactly?"

"This town is Bamburgh, in Northumbria. It's on the coast, just a stone's throw from the holy isle of Lindisfarne."

At this, the castaway's eyes lit up.

"Lindisfarne. I heard tell of its fame. Is there an abbot on the isle?"

"Not an abbot, but a bishop and he is in Durham where the shrine of Saint Cuthbert is venerated."

Conversation ceased as Kenrick served the scalding broth. It worked wonders reviving them both and Thurgot was able to remove the cloak and try to dry out his clothing underneath.

"I cast off my cloak," he explained, "I'm not a swimmer and thought it best."

"Don't worry, there's an old cloak of mine you can have if you're not ashamed to be seen in it! But you'll not need it for a few days. You'll get your strength back here, first."

"You are a good man. Tell me about your life."

Kenrick obliged and it wasn't until he reached the recent past that Thurgot's face changed aspect from interested alertness to sullen anger.

"The Norman swine," he said, at Kenrick's account of the devastation in the north. "Thanks to them I lost my inheritance, too. I'll explain later. You finish now."

He listened attentively to Kenrick's tale of his life after the rebellion and to his dashed hopes of becoming a master mason.

"That will never do," said Thurgot, "your God-given talent is wasted as a labourer. When I recover my strength, I'll use it to help you regain your position."

Kenrick laughed bitterly,

"No offence, friend, but how can a poverty-stricken Saxon help one of his similars?"

He tossed another piece of wood on the fire and said,

"It's your turn; tell me about your life."

Kenrick prided himself on being a good judge of faces and he liked the castaway's appearance. As he heard the tale, he grew increasingly pleased that he'd plunged into the sea to save him. When his guest paused, concerned, he asked him,

"Are you alright? Do you need a drink? I have some mead."

Thinking it might restore him even more, Thurgot accepted, swearing to himself that he'd repay his burly host a thousandfold for his ungrudging kindness.

They grinned at each other as they swallowed the warming liquid.

"So, you were saying, you convinced the captain not to turn back. What was life like for you in Norway?"

"I think God must have had a purpose for me because the king— he's called Olav—took me into his court and had me teach psalm-singing to his people. This will interest you, Kenrick, the king involved me with the construction of some of his churches."

He was right, they exchanged technical details, the mason displaying a deep interest in the round piers and moulded plinths that Thurgot described. The eyes of the survivor lit up with a fervid glow in the dancing firelight,

"I think God had a purpose with that shipwreck. He meant for you to save me, else why were you on the beach in such filthy weather? My task is to help you create something like those churches here in Northumbria. He explained,

"You would have learnt so much in Nidaros. The piers were reeded and cylindrical with scalloped capitals. The mason told me he had been on pilgrimage and seen similar ones in Syria. When the time is right, I'll sketch them for you, Kenrick—and you will build them."

Again, the mason laughed, but this time, his chortle wasn't mocking but contained hope.

SEVEN

EVESHAM ABBEY, MARCH 1073

PRIOR ALDWYN STROLLED GAZING AROUND INTO THE courtyard of Evesham Abbey. Strange to relate, since the two abbeys, his own at Winchcombe and this one stood only ten miles apart, he'd never set foot there. He had obtained permission from his stern and vigorous Norman abbot, Galandus, to embark on a much longer journey if and only if he could convince others from Evesham to join him in seclusion. The task of convincing was no easy one as his abject failure in his own monastery demonstrated. What the prior was asking of would-be companions was extreme self-denial.

True to his ideals, he relegated his thirst and tiredness to the back of his mind and hesitated only long enough to have a curious monk accost him,

"Are you lost, brother, whom is it you seek?"

The friendly tone and smile heartened Aldwyn.

"Hardly lost, my friend, for I come only from beyond the hills to the south, from my abbey at Winchcombe. But I must speak with your abbot. What name does he go by?"

Momentarily, the pleasant smiling face clouded and Aldwyn

thought he heard *the stickler* mumbled, but was unsure. Recovering his former cheerful air, the monk smiled again and said,

"It is Abbot Aethelwig. If you are on an errand of importance, he's the man for you; if not, I fear you should seek someone else—the prior, maybe?"

Aldwyn was perturbed but since his mission qualified as important to his mind, decided to go ahead with his original plan.

"Tell me, what is the disposition of the abbot?"

The monk looked worried and scrutinised the newcomer's face. He did not want trouble and knew not who this inquisitive stranger was or what he was about. Talkative and helpful by nature, the brother swallowed hard and determined to be useful without compromising himself.

"Best if you find out for yourself, brother, I'll just say that the abbot is a good Christian and justly demands high standards of discipline from our community."

"That is as it should be. Do you think he will receive a traveller here on God's business?"

"I'll take you to his quarters and he'll decide. But don't be surprised if he keeps you waiting or refuses to see you at all."

The monk led the way but had grown strangely silent. Aldwyn considered that the fellow was ensuring that no criticism would be levelled at him. At last, his guide spoke,

"Who shall I say is seeking the Father Abbot?"

"Tell him Prior Aldwyn of Winchcombe begs an audience."

Despite the earlier warning, Aldwyn was admitted to the presence of an elderly, white-haired monk of austere appearance.

"Thank you, brother, you may leave us," thus he dismissed Aldwyn's cheerful guide, but he frowned and stared at the door that the brother had carelessly left slightly ajar. He clicked his tongue and strode over to close it. He said over his shoulder,

"I gather you are prior at Winchcombe, a place dear to me, for I was in charge there for three years before the present incumbent."

"Abbot Galandus is a worthy spiritual leader to us, Father."

Aethelwig gave him an appraising stare and smiled,

"Ay, his reputation for intelligence and shrewdness has reached us. But come, you are not here for idle chatter. What brings you to Evesham?"

"My superior has released me from my vow of stability, for my heart burns with desire to imitate the great saints of Northumbria: Aidan, Cuthbert, Coelfrith and Bede—"

"Ah, indeed? Only lately I read Bede's account of the miracles of Saint Cuthbert. But you set yourself a task of mortification and abnegation if you intend to emulate these shining examples of our faith at its best."

"Father, I am resolved to seek out there the ruined, once-great holy places to live a life of poverty in imitation of the saints I mentioned."

The austere lined countenance became severe and the abbot's tone chiding,

"It would be *as well* that you knew what that truly means. Have you any idea of how Cuthbert lived with only the sky as his companion in a walled-up cell? Are you prepared to lead a life of such denial?"

"That is my intention, Father. But I seek companions who are disposed to share my desire and help rebuild the holy places. I have come to ask permission to address your monks to this purpose."

"I am guessing that you convinced no-one at Winchcombe," the shrewd eyes twinkled.

"You are right, Father."

"No surprise, when you are offering nought but a hard life of sacrifice."

"Ay, but in return for a life of eternal splendour."

The head of the abbey chortled and to Aldwyn's astonishment, laid a hand on each shoulder and scanned his features at close quarters. The pale blue, slightly watery eyes regarded him as though wanting to memorise them forever. Satisfied, the elderly monk removed his right hand, made the sign of the cross and leaving his left firmly on his visitor's shoulder, blessed him. When he had finished and released his guest, the abbot declared,

"Prior Aldwyn, I see the Almighty has reserved great deeds to you. Go forth among the brothers and if you persuade any, bring them to me and they, too, will receive my blessing. Go!"

Aldwyn smiled, bowed and was careful to shut the door properly. He stood outside in the courtyard and thought,

Why is it that the abbot did not gather the brothers and tell them my purpose?

He frowned, leant against the wall, placing the sole of a sandal against it.

I know! It's a test. He expects me to have the wit and desire to do this alone. And in that he's right!

Aldwyn pondered for a while and as he considered what to do because he had no authority to call a meeting, but noticed the curious looks of monks as they passed him by. That gave him an idea. Slipping down until he was seated against the wall, he did not move and began to meditate. The hours went by and still, he was motionless. Only by happy chance, the wall he had chosen was sheltered from the cool south-westerly wind. Vaguely, he saw the weak evening shadows cast by the low March sun lengthen. One or two of the brothers were pointing towards him, which was exactly what he had hoped for but none of them approached him. The night was long and cold but he did not budge.

At five o'clock in the morning, the first faint light hinted at the birth of day and with it came the monks to Lauds to recite the dawn prayers. Through lowered eyes, he peered at them—the first people he had seen for three long hours when he'd watched their backs disappear indoors after Matins. That was their nightly sacrifice known also as *Vigil*, but in truth, nobody was suffering as much as he in his cramping veritable solitary vigil. That he had been noticed now at sunrise where certainly he had gone unnoticed in the depths of the night, was clear from the brothers' reactions. Even so, to his bitter disappointment, not a soul came to him to ask what he was about.

The solemn reserve of the monks was broken after Prime, two hours later. On finding the strange monk dressed in a habit similar to their own, still slumped against the wall after an afternoon, evening and night without movement, they surrendered to their curiosity. Rather like a flock of sheep, following its leader, they trailed after the cheerful monk who, on his arrival had taken him to the abbot. This fellow, in his usual jovial manner, remembering the visitor's station, said,

"Prior, why is it that you suffer so against a comfortless wall?"

"In the name of our Lord, how my legs ache! I fear I can no longer stand. Who will help me rise? I must speak with you, brothers."

They helped him and witnessed the pain it caused him merely to gain his feet. Nobody wanted to miss the reason underlying this mortification.

Aldwyn began by praising Cuthbert and in a stronger voice than he thought he could muster after his physical trials, described the saint's life as a hermit and justly declared that if he had suffered for one night seated by the wall, what must the saint have undergone in his isolation on Farne? He invited them to think about that and then went on to relate how the saint had restored sight to a blind man and other miracles.

"Is there nobody among you who will come with me? Brothers I leave for the land of Cuthbert and I will lead a life of poverty there but I need like-minded fellows to be with me to restore the holy places. Have no fear. Abbot Aethelwig will give his blessing to anyone who so desires."

"That I will, right gladly..."

All heads turned to stare at the smiling abbot at the back of the assembled monks. His surreptitious arrival had gone unnoticed by everyone, even Aldwyn, who was facing in the right direction to have noticed but had been too intent on his speech.

"But know this, brothers, whoever goes with Prior Aldwyn must not be faint-hearted," continued the abbot, "but prepared to endure the torments of the flesh as did our Redeemer for us."

His tone was grave and doubtful but Aldwyn appreciated his intervention. A low murmur of voices was accompanied with glances cast in the direction of the prior and the occasional gesture. As the monks began to drift away, Aldwyn's heart sank. Failure once again! And after a night of useless agony. Why had God abandoned him? Was his idea to emulate his spiritual heroes born of false pride? Tormenting himself with such thoughts, he went to retrieve his ass from the stables. The donkey served to carry liturgical books that he had accumulated and vestments on his long and, now it appeared, lone journey.

Downcast, he led the faithful beast towards the gates when the robust figure of the cheerful monk came hastening towards him. Red-faced from the exertion of a fifty-yard charge, the brother puffed and gasped, making Aldwyn smile.

"You deserve a beaker of a fine vintage after your efforts, my friend. But why the hurry?"

The monk's eyes brightened at the thought of wine but he had a message to deliver.

"Father Abbot asks you to go at once to his quarters on a matter of urgency. You may leave Brother Ass here with me," he said, delicately stroking the donkey's muzzle.

Puzzled, but with hope springing in his bosom, Aldwyn knocked on the abbot's door.

"Enter!"

To his delight, he saw two monks kneeling before the abbot's small corner altar, normally reserved for the abbot's worship, he assumed. The nearest of the two to him had the muscular build of a warrior. But had they decided to accompany him? The abbot ended his uncertainty at once.

"Prior, God has heeded your plea and the spirit has moved these two brothers to follow your example. Stand brethren!" The two monks rose, making the sign of the cross, bowed and turned to face the abbot.

"This is Elfwy, a deacon, and he..." he pointed to the muscular fellow, "...is Reinfrid, a novice and..." he added with distaste, "...a *Norman* warrior." Abbot Aethelwig of Saxon stock made no effort to disguise his preferences. "They are moved to join you, Prior, thus, I hereby revoke their vows of stability and appoint you, Prior Aldwyn, as their superior. They are bound to obey you in all things. I presume that is clear to you, brothers?"

"Ay."

"Ay, Father Abbot."

"Good. Then go with my blessing. Follow in the footsteps of Saint Cuthbert and you cannot be misled by the Evil One. Ah, Prior, one last thing. As you approach the Humber, go to the abbey at Selebie and there seek Abbot Benoit—or as I believe he calls himself now, Benedict. Tell him you visit him in the name of his friendship with Abbot Aethelwig and explain your mission. He will aid you. Bless you, my sons! In the name of the Father..."

They collected the donkey and set off on their long and arduous journey. The wearying tramp across Mercia towards the Humber was uneventful. Occasional well-wishers pressed dried fruit or bread on them but they proceeded unmolested. Aldwyn knew that the problem of outlaws was more real north of the great estuary. Was that why Abbot Aethelwig had insisted on their visit to the abbey at Selebie?

His intuition proved correct. The abbot, a spiritual Frenchman, was deeply affected by their mission and provided them with practical assistance, summoning the sheriff of Yorkshire, Hugh fitzBaldric, who swore to guide them with an escort across the dangerous moorland as far as the land of Cuthbert.

They set off on their journey and the sheriff, looking back at the abbey, made Aldwyn turn around and pointed out the banner flying over the abbey gateway. It was a blue flag with three white swans emblazoned.

"Do you know the tale of that emblem, Prior?"

"I do not," Aldwyn confessed, at the same time, curious to know and glad to while away the tedious march in conversation. He had wondered about the strange crest, being unable to recall an episode in the Bible referring to three swans. He told the sheriff as much and received hearty laughter in reply.

"That is because there is none such, brother. Hark! I'll tell you the tale. You've met Abbot Benedict. When he was a monk in France at the abbey of Auxerre, he had a vision in which the founder, Saint Germain, told him to build an abbey in Yorkshire. The good monk, unwilling to transfer to a foreign land, dismissed the episode as a dream and ignored it, but on having the same experience twice more, upped and left his homeland. Benedict was certain in his calling and departed from the Abbey in the middle of the night with Germain's finger in a golden box as a relic. The vision had instructed him to search for *a place called Selby, provided for my honour, ordained for worship, destined for future fame and situated on the banks of the River Ouse, not far from York—*"

"And so, he founded the abbey at Selebie?"

"He did not, Prior! Nay, his knowledge of our country was so poor that he ended up in Salisbury."

Aldwyn laughed,

"Salisbury!"

"Ay, so, redirected, he journeyed by ship to Kings Lynn with an interpreter Theobald, and from there caught a cargo vessel for York via the Humber. Then he saw, in reality, the swans of his vision at a bend of the Ouse near the marshy hamlet of Selebie."

By now, the other two brothers had been captivated by the tale and Elfwy said,

"So that explains the banner with three swans."

"It does, ay."

"Because Benedict founded the abbey right there," Reinfrid joined in.

"Hold! It was not that easy," the sheriff wished to milk his tale to the full, "the area that Benedict chose was slightly higher than the surrounding terrain, which as you saw was very flat and was a site already marked out as an important meeting place. In that place grew a great oak tree given the name *Strihac*, where the people held moots, with the land around it owned by the King. Benedict set up a wooden cross and a simple shelter made out of branches and leaves there. That's where I came in, for it was my duty as sheriff to inform King William, who was celebrating Christmas in York. By fortunate coincidence, a few months earlier, the king's fourth son, Henry, was born in that same place."

"And so, the king gave Benedict permission to build his abbey," said Aldwyn, enjoying the tale.

"Precisely, because it seemed like an omen to the king—the exact place his son was born. Not only that, but he also gave him the vills of Flaxley, Brayton and Rawcliffe so that he would have the income to start building."

They marched on cheerfully, going beyond York and heading into the area with the worse reputation for outlaw activity. After a period of long silence, the sheriff started to converse again,

"See, up there, Prior, yon forest? Well, that was where Swain and his band of scoundrels hid and whence they defied the law. Once Abbot Benedict had built his abbey and the people of the surrounding area had contributed to it, the villain was drawn with the ill intent to make off with the abbey silver. To rob the wealth of the monastery, he came with his men at night. Do you know what happened?" He paused for effect but getting no answer, continued, "when he tried to lift the door off its hinges, God caused Swain's hand to stick to the wall. Nothing he could do would free it. Think of that! He was trapped there until Benedict arrived in the morning and only when he confessed his crimes and begged for repentance was his hand freed. The forests and the heathland hereabouts are still infested with outlaws, which is why these stout lads are armed and ready to wield their weapons to ensure your safety, Prior.

Luckily, they were not called upon to fight and the small party arrived in Dearthington, where the sheriff and his men left them to worship in Saint Cuthbert's church.

On the steps of the church, Hugh fitzBaldric said,

"About another eight leagues, Prior, and you'll be in Durham. You'll be safe enough for the rest of your journey. He quoted from the Book of Proverbs to the astonishment of the monks: *Look straight ahead, and fix your eyes on what lies before you. Mark out a straight path for your feet; stay on the safe path.*"

Aldwyn, who was impressed by the layman's knowledge of the scriptures, realising at once that the sheriff was no ordinary official, gave him a grateful smile and said,

"Farewell, bless you for your guidance thus far, know that our eyes verily are fixed on what lies ahead of us."

EIGHT

DURHAM AND JARROW, APRIL 1074

THURGOT HAD FORMED A FIRM FRIENDSHIP WITH KENRICK, quite apart from owing him his life, he found that he had much in common with the gentle giant. Aware that he had outstayed his welcome, he felt obliged to leave, not that Kenrick showed any discontent at his presence, the opposite if anything. But he was not contributing to food and the desire to get on with his life was compelling.

"My friend, it is time for me to seek the Bishop of Durham, folk say that he is as spiritual a leader as a prelate should be. I wish to meet him and offer my clerical skills. Thanks to you, I have regained my strength."

Kenrick did not attempt to conceal his feelings. He had grown fond of his lodger and learnt much from their conversations, so with a sorrowful tone, he pleaded,

You know I like having you here. Why don't you stay and find work at the earl's castle?"

"They say that the earl is rebellious by nature and not in the king's graces. If we are to achieve our dreams, Kenrick, we must choose our allegiances carefully."

"Are you still clinging to the foolish idea that I'll ever be anything else other than a mason's labourer, fit only to mix and carry mortar—and you more than a humble scrivener?"

"I sense that God has different plans for us, my friend. You will see. And the first step is to see Bishop Walcher."

"Well, since you insist on speaking for both of us, I'll come with you to Durham."

"You will! The Lord be praised!"

A strange expression clouded Kenrick's visage even in the face of his friend's joy,

"Any fool can do my work here." He growled this so low that Thurgot was unsure whether he'd heard aright. The mason continued in a louder, mocking voice, "Anyway, it's nigh on twenty-four leagues to Durham from here, goodness knows, with your knack for running into rocks..."

They both laughed and Thurgot said,

"When can we leave? Don't you have people to tell and rent to pay?"

"I'll tell my master that I've finished there and if he's honest, he'll give me my week's wages. Then, I'll give the rent to the widow." He was referring to the good woman who rented him the rooms. "She'll find another tenant easily enough. There's a shortage of places to stay in Bamburgh."

Everything in order, they set off south before noon and, keeping a decent pace, taking turns to share Kenrick's horse—how he loved that animal, never once having considered selling it—they reached a large farmstead by the River Aln comfortably before twilight. Kenrick cheered up at the sight of the dairy cattle because he still had a few coins in his purse after paying his dues.

"Here, we can buy cheese and milk, Brother." He called Thurgot *brother* teasingly but with genuine fondness, "and if we're lucky, they'll let us sleep in a barn on the hay. Our Smoca will eat and drink too, she deserves a treat." He jerked a thumb at the dappled smoke-grey mare.

This all went pleasantly to plan because the Anglian farmer, who had lost his land to a Norman overlord and whose products contributed to the swelling De Tesson coffers, welcomed a Saxon and an Anglian wayfarer with open arms. He accepted a fair price for bread, cheese and milk but threw in winter apples and honey cake at no extra charge. This they ate by a small fire that he prepared for them in a barn, warning, "Do not add wood. I'll not have you burning my byre down! Besides, the air's mild now that *Eostremonath* is drawing to a close, so you'll be warm enough on the hay, he pointed to a raised wooden platform where he stored his bales.

"We're on our way to Durham, friend," Kenrick informed the farmer, "how much farther from here?"

The ceorl scratched his short blond hair and looked at Smoca munching the hay he'd provided,

"I can't be sure, but I reckon you've another seventeen leagues or so from here. With just one horse, you'll not make it in the day, tomorrow. My guess is you'll be pressed to reach the Tyne before nightfall, but," he calculated, "ay, you ought to get there if you set off early, say an hour after the first cock crows when I'll bring you fresh milk. Good night to you. I have to fetch in the cows."

"I'll help," said Kenrick, leaping up.

"No need, I do it every day," he grinned at the travellers.

Since they had decided to travel due south, they were never far from the coast and so, they reached the Tyne the next evening at a place called Mununceaster and there, they found a tavern with a stable for the mare and two pallets with straw mattresses, good enough to provide rest for their weary bones. The plain fare and the watery ale were cheap but sufficient to restore their strength and knowing that the next morning should see them reach Durham by noon if they set off again at first cock call, and if the innkeeper was right, meant they slept easily.

Their journey had been uneventful thus far, but the road ran through woodland. It made Kenrick uneasy and he was glad his turn to mount Smoca had come, for the outlook from horseback is different from that gained on foot. That was why he saw the outlaws before Thurgot.

"Let's be having your purse," a scar-faced bearded rogue, mounted on an undernourished nag, cried. Behind him, three other scoundrels— two, sat on what looked like wild, moorland ponies to Kenrick's expert eye— glowered and swung cudgels menacingly.

Kenrick laughed, drawing out his meagre bag of coins, knowing he was down to his last pittance.

"You've chosen badly, miserable whoreson!"

He tossed the slim purse to the villain, who caught it deftly, sneering as he squeezed it to feel the contents.

"I think not!" he drew a knife from his belt, "yon horse is worth our trouble lads."

Kenrick did not possess a sword but he never travelled without his seax. Drawing it, he nudged Smoca forward. He would rather die than surrender his beloved dappled-grey mare. Thurgot had brought a sturdy staff to lean on during his travels and although he was no warrior, he had learnt to wield a stave in his youth. The leader of the outlaws charged but his wicked blade was shorter than Kenrick's seax and the mason, a taller man by a head, had a longer reach. So, the first exchange brought a scream from the scoundrel as Kenrick's well-honed edge slashed across his arm, causing him to drop his weapon. The other three outlaws bore down on Kenrick, heavy cudgels raised, little caring that their leader was incapacitated. Their desire for the lovely dapple-grey horse made them reckless. A fatal mistake was to ignore Thurgot, whose staff whacked across the rump of the lead horse, causing it to rear and unseat its rider, leaving him vulnerable to a mighty crack on the head from the same stave. Odds of two against two made one of the villains hesitate, freeing Kenrick to slice the hand of the first cudgel-wielding outlaw. On seeing his comrade disabled, too, the last rider wheeled his steed and galloped away into the forest. But Kenrick had not finished with the bleeding wretch that he had disarmed. As far as he was concerned, the tables were now completely turned. The moorland pony was a hardy creature and it would serve for Thurgot. He seized the reins with one hand and raising his seax with the other, roaring,

"Down! Or I'll take your head off your shoulders!"

Having already sampled the keenness of the menacing blade, clutching his deeply wounded hand, the wretch slid to the ground.

"Brother, take his purse, his fellow thief took mine; so, after all, the exchange is fair."

Thurgot grinned and ripped the bag dangling from the villain's belt before obeying Kenrick's order to mount the pony.

They arrived in Durham two hours earlier than hoped where they discovered that the outlaw's purse, though hardly bulging, contained two stolen pieces of silver and smaller coins, which meant they could afford for their horses to be pampered and that they, too, could eat a decent stew and buy more than one well-brewed ale.

Thoroughly refreshed, they obtained information about the new residence of the bishop since the old one had been burnt to the ground, as Kenrick knew well. So, they asked for and gained admission and, to their surprise, found the prelate a genial person. Kenrick was able to tell him about his masonic skills and the plans he had shared with his predecessor, Ethelwin. With a sorrowful expression, the bishop explained that there was no money for such an ambitious plan. Instead, the king had commanded him to ensure the building of a castle on the hill and all funds would be directed to this in the foreseeable future. But the bishop's eyes lit up as an idea occurred to him.

"Your arrival here is another example of divine providence, my sons. You," he smiled at Thurgot, "are a cleric and wish to become a monk. You, Kenrick, are a mason... and I have news for you both. Of late, I have sent a most worthy prior and his companions to the ancient ruined monastery where our venerable predecessor, Bede, lived and wrote his learned tomes. I speak of Jarrow, where those three brothers live and worship in a roofless ruin. If ever a builder was needed to restore the edifice it is there, where the church of St Paul was set on fire and destroyed by King William's troops. It will be your task, my friend, to rebuild the church and the monastery—some of the old walls are still standing—"

"But, Your Grace, what about money for the materials and the labourers?"

The bishop gave a secretive smile and Kenrick saw the whites of his eyes as he gazed heavenwards as if in supplication.

His voice was emotional when he spoke,

"Before long, my circumstances, thanks be to God, will have changed. But I cannot speak of this today. Just let me say that by the time you are ready to begin work, Master Kenrick, the coin will be forthcoming. As for you, Thurgot, I am sending you to Prior Aldwyn and if he judges you favourably, as I do, there is no better man to prepare you for the monk's habit. Meanwhile, you will act as clerk to him and obey him as your superior."

The bishop smiled, stepped over to a strongbox, took out some silver coins and gave them to Thurgot. This small sum will help you on your journey to Jarrow. It is but six leagues to the northeast. At this hour, you will need lodgings for tonight but you ought to arrive comfortably on the morrow.

They returned to the tavern where their horses were still stabled, paid for another night and took a room for themselves, but first, downstairs chatting excitedly over beakers of ale about Jarrow.

"We can eat here again, it wasn't bad food at midday, was it?" Thurgot said.

"Ay, why not? I was thinking. You, who understand bishops, kings and all, what do you think Walcher meant when he said *my situation will have changed?* I mean, he's bishop here and he didn't sound like he was going to York or Canterbury to become archbishop."

Thurgot chortled, frowned and said,

"I believe he has the means to gain more power. Quite how, I'm not sure, but he sounded confident. I'm sure he will give you the money to repair the church at Jarrow."

They chatted about their plans and the speculations they had about the prior they would meet, agreeing that the bishop held him in high esteem because he had mentioned the prior's *love and his deeds*.

Kenrick suddenly looked thoughtful, pulled at his beard and said,

"Brother, remember the day we met... under rather wet circumstances...you told me that you'd help me regain my position? Well, odd as it may seem, this might well be the first step for us. What do you think?"

"Oh, there's no doubt in my mind. When you spoke to the bishop about the new cathedral, did you see his face? If he had the money, he would start on it tomorrow. One day, Kenrick! Just be patient! It seems your first labour will be in honour of Saint Paul."

"That's if we ever make it to Jarrow."

"What do you mean?"

"We have to go north again— and you saw what happened this morning."

"Ay, I gained a horse and two silver coins."

Kenrick guffawed, and slapped a thigh,

"So, you did! Maybe you'll take a Viking longship!"

They ate another acceptable meal and animatedly discussed their respective futures until weariness urged them to retire. Kenrick said,

"Brother, our destiny begins tomorrow."

"Probably more than you suspect, my friend."

NINE

JARROW, NORTHUMBRIA 1074 AD

Prior Aldwyn beamed at Kenrick and Thurgot.

"You are truly welcome to this holy place, brothers. As you can see, it was once a great monastery. It was here that the saintly Bede came as a boy of seven and stayed until his death more than fifty years later. He wrote his *Historia* here," he said this in an awed tone and shared his confidence with them, "You know, it was reading his *Ecclesiastical History of the English People* that inspired me to come here, to lead a life of poverty and to revive the fortunes of the abbey."

"It's not much more than a ruin," Kenrick grumbled.

"Ay, Master Mason, but there's stone aplenty for you to work with. The Vikings attacked the monastery second only after Lindisfarne then they came back and destroyed it completely in 860. The brothers were forced to abandon the ruins. What do you say to rebuilding the abbey, brother?"

"I say I'll need men with calloused hands, strong backs and thighs, used to heaving and mixing. Not monks who spend their lives on their knees in prayer."

Prior Aldwyn smiled sweetly,

"None of us shuns hard toil, Master Kenrick. You command and we will work until we drop."

"That's what I'm afraid of," Kenrick mumbled under his breath but then, in a louder voice said, "Bishop Walcher promised me coin and I have some silver I can use to bring one or two labourers. But all in good time, we must consider what is needed."

"First, brother, we must rebuild one of the two churches. The old monks had a funerary chapel attached to the main church, see, over there."

"I can build a church on the same spot," Kenrick said after inspecting the ruin, "we can use the original foundations here and here. It will save much work if the building is large enough for you, Prior?" He paced out the length and breadth of the walls and turned,

"Well?"

He saw eagerness on the monk's face,

"That would be magnificent! When can you start?"

"As soon as I have a supply of lime. I expect my first job will be to make a kiln, even a temporary one. Without lime, we have no mortar and without that no building in stone. Then there's the question of water."

"As to that," said Aldwyn eagerly, "there's a well over here and we already have a pail and rope. It is good drinking water but you can use it for mixing your mortar."

Inspection complete, Kenrick, with an anxious expression, turned to Thurgot,

"How do you feel about me selling your horse? You won't need it here and I can raise money for the materials to build the church."

"Given the price I paid for the beast, I'm happy for you to sell it," Thurgot grinned.

"Good, then I'll ride over to the nearest settlement and see what trade I can do."

Without further discussion, he took Smoca and the moorland pony and rode to the fishing village of Hebburn. The small port served him better than he imagined possible because, on the wharf, he found a lime kiln. He studied the construction with great attention, memorising the dimensions and the oval shape of the brick-built oven, the 'eye' underneath to channel the air and noted the metal grid to bear the lime and coal. He knew he could build one exactly like it. The owner clarified why the kiln was on the quay...since it was easier for builders to transport his product by water and he delivered all along the Tyne. Ironically, Kenrick needed the powder to make his lime kiln, so, he bought sufficient for the construction. He explained that he was rebuilding the church at Jarrow, at which news, the man became extremely helpful and promised to deliver the lime and enough brick for the oven that same day.

"You'll need coal and limestone. I can bring that, too. I'll give you a good price."

They discussed business for a while until Kenrick said,

"I don't suppose you know anyone who wants to buy a horse?"

"I wondered why you came with two; that one looks undernourished."

"That's because I've only had her a few days and the previous owner neglected her. But she's doing well now and comes from hardy stock and only four winters behind her."

The trader walked over and inspected the mare's teeth. He looked at Kenrick shrewdly,

"What do you think about giving her to me? In exchange, I'll bring your first two deliveries of coal and limestone at no cost. That's a fair trade."

Kenrick considered a moment,

In that case, I can use the money saved to hire labour.

As was the custom, he spat on his palm and offered his hand to the trader, who clasped it and took the mare's reins to fasten her to a fence post.

"I know where St Paul's monastery is, you'll have your first delivery before sunset."

"Good, well, I'll be on my way. I have to find a carpenter who knows his trade and a labourer looking for work."

"Get you to the smithy, down yon lane. I heard tell the smith's brother is looking for a job."

And I need a smith, anyway.

"Thank you, friend, you've been a great help."

"Anything for the brothers. It's God's work you're about."

Smoke rose in a dark coil from the forge and even as he tied Smoca outside, he felt the heat coming in waves from within.

"Good day to you, traveller," the smutty-faced smith, a man with no eyebrows, laid a pair of tongs on a bench and stepped out to get a welcome breath of air, "Does your horse need shoeing? Fine beast!"

"She does not, but I need to purchase one or two items and to discuss a matter with you. My name's Kenrick, I'm from the monastery at Jarrow and wish to buy a heavy hammer, two shovels and—"

"Ay, discuss a matter with me."

"That's it. And I need you to make me a support grid for a lime kiln. Also, you see, I'm a mason and I'm looking for a skilled carpenter. I heard tell your brother knows that trade. Is he hereabouts?"

The broad-chested ceorl took a deep breath and bellowed like a bull:

"Hailwin!"

From the depths of the forge emerged a muscular individual, a fit match in size for the smith but complete with bushy eyebrows, from which Kenrick deduced that he did not work the furnace.

"What do you want?" the newcomer addressed his brother whilst looking suspiciously at their visitor.

"This here is a mason and he's looking for a carpenter. That's what you did when you were at Hexham, ain't it?"

"Ay, it is so. I'm seeking work but there's none around here."

"I'm looking for a carpenter, but one who can use his head without me constantly having to watch over him."

The burly ceorl looked offended,

"An' who might you be, so high and mighty?"

Kenrick laughed, this was the sort of spirited fellow he could use if he knew his trade.

"I'm a master mason and I work for the monks at Jarrow. I'm going to rebuild St Paul's, the church that the Vikings destroyed. What about you, have you served your time?"

"Ay, as my brother said, I was at Hexham and worked on the new transept of the priory. Learnt a lot there, I did, and I'm a good worker."

Kenrick sized him up, eyes roving over the broad chest, muscular arms and strong thighs.

"You seen enough? I ain't a bloody horse and you ain't looking at my teeth, either!"

Kenrick chortled, he liked the bluff carpenter,

"You'll do for me, Hailwin, as long as you'll make do with the normal rates because the brothers are sworn to poverty and I sold a horse to pay your wages."

The carpenter beamed, "No trouble on that score Master Mason, I'll be glad to be in work again."

They discussed pay to their mutual satisfaction and Kenrick made an instant friend by giving a week's wages in advance. He was happy to do this because the carpenter agreed to bring his own tools and to make the mason a straight-edge with a plumb bob attached."

The smith, who had disappeared into the forge returned bearing two shovels and a heavy-looking lump hammer.

He wielded the tool as if it was a bauble,

"I'm guessing you'll need this for smashing up limestone, am I right?"

"Ay, you are!"

"Well, it's up to you, I can give you one with a long handle if you like, but it's my opinion that this short handle gives you better control."

"I agree. I'm used to a short handle like that and I see you brought the shovels. I came to the right man."

"That you did, Master, also because I'm going to give you a shovel for no charge since you're taking this oaf off my hands and you're about God's work. And I'm assuming you want that grill the same size, and all, as I made for the one on the wharf."

That was splendid news and saved a lot of explanation and trouble. So, Kenrick confirmed at once, adding,

"You are a good man. One last question to both of you. I'll need a sturdy labourer for mixing the mortar. Would you know of anyone?"

"Ha-ha! Boomed the smith, "Radwig!" he thundered. "You might as well take another waster off my hands."

A fresh-faced sturdy youth with a remarkable resemblance to Hailwin but a good ten years younger came running around the corner of the forge.

"Did you call me, Irmgard?"

"How many bloody Radwigs are there around here? Course I called you, clot! Now then, do you or do you not want to earn some wages?"

The young fellow looked eagerly at Kenrick, who could be the only possible source of wages.

"Ay, I do. But I'm no smith."

Kenrick smiled, he had struck lucky with these honest brothers.

"I seek no smith, leastways, I found the one I need," he beamed at Irmgard, "Nay, I'm looking for a strong-armed willing worker to help me mix and carry."

"You can test my arm if you're prepared to be beaten," bragged the cocksure youth.

Eager for sport, the smith took them into his kitchen, offered Kenrick a welcome beaker of his strong home-brewed cider and sat Radwig opposite the mason. Kenrick was a giant of a man and could easily have been born into this family of mighty Anglians. He had no wish to humiliate the young man,

"You have no chance; I'll understand if you withdraw."

"Me? Nay, it's you who'll lose the bout!"

"Let's see if your muscles are as well-developed as your bragging, then!"

They arm-wrestled until beads of sweat appeared on both brows. Kenrick regretted underestimating the strength of the youth and by now his brothers were urging him to try harder. It is a fact that the mind plays an equal part to the arm in such contests and so, Kenrick said softly,

"The lad is strong but he's almost spent."

His words had the desired effect, enraging his opponent into an unwise greater effort, which Kenrick resisted and as soon as the youth stopped the extra effort, shoved down with all his might and broke the resistance to win the contest. He stood in triumph and said,

"No-one *ever* has given me such a close-run battle! You are strong for your age, Radwig, I am pleased you will work on my church. Now we must discuss your pay!"

The sullen expression disappeared at once, to be replaced with a cheerful grin,

"Master, I will come and work with you under one condition,"

Irmgard gave him a ferocious glower that boded ill for the lad, but the youth said,

"On condition that you'll give me another chance to best you at the arm contest."

The smith bellowed a laugh and taunted his brother,

"You'd best wait till the mason is an old man if you want to get the better of him. Now, be off, the lot of you, some of us have work to do."

Kenrick put an arm around the youth's shoulder,

"We'll do it again one day, but I too, have a condition for you,

The lad glanced anxiously at the smith,

"Ay?"

"I want you to carry my hammer to Jarrow, it's awkward for me with the shovels on my horse."

Radwig grinned and nodded,

"I can do that, Master," he picked up the heavy hammer and said,

"I'm going to pack a bag with some clothes and a blanket and I'll be right along."

Since Hailwin was busy gathering carpentry tools into a large canvas pack, Kenrick bade farewell to the smith, who said,

"You've got yourself two good workers there. I don't expect they'll give cause for trouble," he raised his voice as Radwig came back into the forge, "but any bother from either of them, Master Mason, and you just come and let me know so as they'll rue the day! Your grid will be ready tomorrow afternoon."

Kenrick rode away, whistling a cheery air. The brothers would walk together and arrive before nightfall. Ahead on the road, as he approached the monastery, he saw a laden ox-cart creaking, groaning and jostling along the track. When he drew level, he saw the trader of earlier, as good as his word, bringing the lime, bricks and limestone as the first of three loads.

"Did you find your carpenter, Master?"

"Ay, thanks to you, friend! The smith's bother will join us."

"Good news, only the other day Irmgard was moaning that he didn't know what to do with him mooching around the place!"

"I'm hiring the young brother, too."

"Ay, he's a good 'un, you'll not regret it."

They turned into the site of the ruined monastery and the ox-driver said,

"You've got a job on your hands here, right enough!"

"Just you keep your part of the bargain, my friend, and I'll think on the rest!"

"Don't worry, I'll be here tomorrow with the first of two loads of coal and limestone."

Brother Reinfrid, the sturdy former warrior, unbidden, was already throwing hefty limestone rocks into a pile near the cart. Kenrick was pleased. That was the kind of attitude he needed. Prior Aldwyn had come over to see what was happening and took a shovel from the mason.

"Where do you want the lime, Kenrick?"

"It needs to be kept dry, Brother," said the merchant, "which is why I brought those sacks. I didn't fill them myself to save time because I want to get back before nightfall." The prior set about filling a sack with the white powder. "Watch your eyes, Brother, that powder can do mighty harm!" called the trader, handing bricks to Kenrick, who stacked them neatly. When he had finished, he climbed onto the cart and helped Reinfrid finish hurling limestone until the waggon was empty.

This is going to be better than I thought.

Kenrick beamed round him at his willing helpers.

"You'll soon have a church to be proud of, Brothers!"

Aldwyn clapped his hands like a delighted child and glowed with pleasure.

"Come, we should all pray that the Lord helps our mason!"

"Well, it seems he has today," Kenrick said with satisfaction. He thought about the smith's siblings. They had said they knew the way; he shouldn't worry yet about their failure to appear because they had heavy tools to carry and the road was long and he'd done it on horseback. They would be here before nightfall.

Reinfrid is a pleasant surprise. We'll work much better than I feared this morning.

He was giving himself to these thoughts instead of following Aldwyn's service in front of the rough wooden cross the brothers had raised before their arrival. Thurgot, though, seemed to understand and follow the strange language of the worship. Suddenly, his fine voice burst into song along with Aldwyn and the two monks. It was a psalm, Kenrick recognised as much, but didn't know the words—just as long as God was happy and continued smiling on him, that was all that mattered.

It seemed that the Almighty was truly benevolent with him because the two brothers, Hailwin, particularly weary from hefting his heavy tools, tramped into the monastery grounds, looking uncertainly around.

"This way!" called Prior Aldwyn. "We have no guest rooms, we're all camping. But I'll understand if you wish to find lodgings in the village."

"Nay, brother..."

"He's *Prior* Aldwyn," Thurgot pointed out.

The carpenter looked embarrassed and tried again.

"I was saying, Prior, what's good for you is good for us, isn't it Radwig?"

The younger brother did not hesitate,

"Ay, no problem for me."

"Good fellows," Aldwyn smiled, "the Lord will look with favour upon you."

"At any rate, Prior, give us a week to sort out a wood supply, and I'll soon knock up a shelter for when the bad weather comes."

They lit a fire and Elfwy, the self-appointed cook set about preparing a simple meal of eel soup, while Kenrick explained how he would build a lime kiln the next day. He just needed to find sand and clay for the mortar.

"There's plenty of sand just over a league to the east—that's why they call the village *Sand*haven!" Hailwin chuckled."

"Splendid! We'll hire a cart and load it with sand. What about clay?"

Radwig surprised them all, especially his brother,

"No problem," he beamed at the mason, "this monastery is built close to where two rivers join, the Don and the Tyne. Where they flow together is where I used to go fishing. Do you remember, Hailwin? I'd come home with flatfish, right? Well, I'd dig up worms for bait and the soil over there, where the rivers meet, is all clay. I'll wager it's what you want, Master."

"You can show me tomorrow morning bright and early before we go to Sandhaven, Radwig."

Everything was falling into place. It seemed too good to be true, but it was enough to provide Kenrick with a good night's sleep.

TEN

JARROW, NORTHUMBRIA, JUNE 1076-78 AD

P<small>EERING OVER THE NEW COURSE OF STONES HE HAD LAID</small>—
blocks he had pillaged from the nearby ancient Roman fort of Sege-
dunum—Kenrick watched with satisfaction as the monks processed
out of Terce from the church of St Paul, which he had constructed
with his own hands. Three months previously, Bishop Walcher had
come to Jarrow to consecrate the edifice and it had been the proudest
moment of his life. The changes the monastery had seen in two years
were largely due to his efforts but this was the visible, physical
restructuring. Arguably the most important change was spiritual.
Word had spread throughout the land that Prior Aldwyn was leading
the revival of Bede's holy abbey and monks had poured in, especially
from the south, to be part of the fledgling community. The influx
provided Kenrick with more willing hands when needed.

To accommodate them, the mason had replaced Hailwin's invaluable wooden shelter, which had served them so well in the first harsh
winter, with a stone guesthouse that included a dormer and still
unfinished refectory. Aldwyn had begged him to give priority to the
kitchen that he was working on now. He detached his gaze from the
file of monks only to focus on his straight-edge and swear. The lead

bob had stopped swinging but the string was not true to the vertical
notch that ran from the raised semi-circle to the bottom edge of the
level. A few coarse words, a heavy sigh and he worked five stones free
from the fresh mortar and scraped at it with his trowel. Replacing his
stones, he patted them down and checked with the straight-edge
again, grunting in satisfaction: perfect! How many times had he done
this on *his* church? He looked with pride once more at the bell tower
and his expert eye could see no imperfection in the neat rows of
stone. Blessed level! Hailwin had made it for him in their first week in
Jarrow and he would have been lost without it. The carpenter had
also made the horseshoe-shaped tool with plumb bob, whose two
'feet' he used to ascertain vertical straightness. Without that instrument, his walls might lean inwards or outwards and that would never
do. Dear Hailwin! Looking back, Kenrick thought, the carpenter had
proved to be his finest recruit. Hadn't he constructed the palisade and
gates to enclose the whole monastery and keep their animals from
straying?

Even as he thought this, Kenrick had to shoo an inquisitive goose
by flicking a foot at it. The creature arched its neck and hissed at him.

Don't worry, I'll roast you at Christmas!

There were goats, sheep and two cows apart from the geese, all in
the care of Brother Drutmund, who had come from Winchester and
who, before losing his farm to the Normans and taking his vows, had
been a farmer in Hampshire. The same monk had created the
vegetable plot now being worked by two brothers straight after Terce.

"Kenrick, Kenrick! The Lord be praised!"

Prior Aldwyn, in a clear state of agitation, came running towards
him in odd contrast with his normal sedate manner of walking in
contemplation.

"News from Durham, Master! Bishop Walcher is so pleased with
what he saw at consecration that he has endowed us with the vill of
Jarrow and its dependencies! What's more, Kenrick, he has made
over to us the church of St Oswin at Tynemouth. You do understand
what this means?"

He scrutinised the perplexed face of the giant builder and saw the confusion, but did not expect the words:

"Ay, more responsibilities for you, Prior."

That was true enough and because of his joy, he had not yet thought of that aspect.

"What it means, dear friend, is that we will no longer have to be sustained by alms from the faithful but have money from tributes that would otherwise have gone to the Church coffers in Durham. Surely, we can finish our project here! Thanks be to God!" The prior believed this when he spoke but life is full of twists and turns. Kenrick reflected,

"True enough, I still have to pay for the last cartload of limestone —it'll save us from having to make the tough overland journey to Wallsend. The stone there, which I'm using now," he tamped down another one, "comes free and sometimes already dressed, but it costs us much in time and fatigue."

"Ah, there's other important news that may also affect us. The messenger told me of the death of Earl Waltheof. He was beheaded as a traitor on St Giles's Hill in Winchester."

"But wasn't he married to the king's niece?"

"Ay, to Judith, but King William tired of his involvement in conspiracies and had him executed."

"Another Saxon earl is gone," Kenrick said bitterly.

The Prior, a Saxon, himself, understood the mason's sentiment and had news to cheer him.

"What you don't know, brother, is that Bishop Walcher is made the new Earl of Northumbria!"

He said this with a triumphant air.

"What? Bishop and Earl all vested in one man?"

"It would appear so and must be good for us. I have heard that the bishop plans to introduce monks into the cathedral chapter and has found masons for the monastic buildings. As for us, it means you will be able to proceed with my dream of a central cloister, Benedictine-style, with an enclosed walkway where the brothers can walk, pray and contemplate. There you are, you see, Kenrick, God sees and provides!"

"Amen!"

He watched the joyful monk retreat and wished he had even half the faith of the prior. He also cursed under his breath. The Prior wanted too much. How would he finish the refectory if he had to build a cloister? He looked back at the church and smiled—anything was possible, all in good time.

But time was the one thing Aldwyn was not prepared to concede. A man with a vision, he considered the growing number of monks at Jarrow, contemplated the resurrection of the structure and made a decision. Other deserted monasteries would benefit from a similar revival, so, in the plant month of August, he called a meeting and outlined his intention.

My cloister's only half-finished and the refectory too. And he wants me to start again on some other blessed ruin.

Whereas Kenrick was unhappy, Elfwy was delighted because Aldwyn appointed him as prior at Jarrow. Reinfrid left that day for Whitby, where he meant to settle as a hermit among the ruins of St Hild's abbey.

Hailwin and Radwig came to see him after the meeting of the monks as they had sensed the excitement of the brothers.

"Master, is it true that you and the prior are leaving Jarrow to start work on another monastery?"

"That's what's happening, ay," growled Kenrick unhappily.

The brothers exchanged glances,

"Well, we're coming with you then!" Radwig blurted.

The mason looked at them as a father would his beloved sons but then frowned,

"I don't even know where the prior intends to go. But if you two scoundrels are coming, I guess I'll sleep better!"

They all grinned and set about their work with a renewed will.

It was Thurgot who put Kenrick's mind truly at ease.

"Listen, friend, I told you God had plans for you. Well, you have impressed the prince-bishop with your skills at Jarrow; now, you'll show him your talent at Melrose."

"Melrose? Is that where he's going? It's a long way from here."

"True, but it's still within Bishop Walcher's diocese."

"Are you sure about that?"

"Certain."

Kenrick shrugged and slapped mortar on top of another stone, wondering if he'd finish the kitchen before they left. This was the last wall, so he might take a stand over it. Seeing his determination and unhappiness, Aldwyn conceded the three days he needed.

"After all, Father Prior, all these monks need a proper kitchen and as it is, I'm leaving them an unfinished cloister, the north wall is missing."

"Don't worry, master, someone else will complete it," the prior reassured him.

But no one ever did.

Hailwin built a handcart to carry his and Kenrick's tools to Melrose but Thurgot insisted that he chose the strongest among the monastery's four donkeys to pull it.

So, they set off on the long journey, Kenrick allowing his companions to ride Smoca in turns. As they approached Melrose, Aldwyn grew ever more enthusiastic, telling anyone who would pay attention that the wide winding river was the Tweed.

When they saw the abandoned monastery, nestling in its enchanting position in a loop of the river, he was beside himself with joy, blurting,

"Behold! What a beautiful secluded place! It was chosen by Saint Aidan with the guidance of the Holy Spirit! Now we shall bring it back to life!"

Thurgot, too, was delighted and added,

"Here it was that Saint Cuthbert first wore the habit of a monk in 651. We follow in his saintly footsteps."

Only Kenrick sighed deeply when he saw the ruinous state of the place. He would have to build another lime kiln to start over again.

Thanks to the skills of the mason and the carpenter, the small brotherhood did not suffer unduly the rigours of the first winter in Melrose and with the arrival of another spring, came the restructuring of much of the monastery. The summer brought an influx of spiritual and intellectual adventurers but, above all, from Kenrick's point of view, more willing muscles.

One day, a messenger arrived from Gospatric, the former earl of Northumbria, who had sought refuge north of the Tweed in 1073. The nobleman had now fallen seriously ill and hearing that Aldwyn and Thurgot were *living in poverty of goods and spirit at Melrose,* summoned them to hear his confession before he died. They offered him comfort and, out of gratitude, he donated two fine ornamental hangings for the altar. One was beautifully embroidered showing a pelican with its young and the other with a mandorla around Christ in ascension.

When Kenrick saw them, bluff as ever, he growled,

"What's the point of a bloody pelican on an altar?"

Thurgot swiftly intervened,

"They say the pelican feeds its young with its blood, so what better symbol, Master Mason, of self-sacrifice for the eucharist?"

Kenrick looked shame-faced as Thurgot only used his formal title when annoyed with him,

"I suppose so," he conceded, looking admiringly at his friend, whose extensive knowledge of everything, never ceased to amaze him. "What about the other, then? I can see that's Christ."

"It is. Ascending to heaven. See, that almond shape surrounding Him, Kenrick? That's a *mandorla,* which means almond in Latin, you know, the nut. It's in the shape of an almond and represents a halo all around His body, not just the head, see?"

"I do! Well, I never! There's so much I don't know."

Kenrick hung his head and looked abashed,

"Ay, but *I* couldn't build a church as you can, my friend, not even for the love of God."

The weeks passed into months and contact with the former earl brought problems for Aldwyn and Thurgot. King Malcolm of Scotland learnt of their presence and was unhappy at foreigners settling on his border, fearing that one day the ill-intentioned might use their presence as a pretext for invasion. With this in mind, he demanded an oath of allegiance, which they refused. Worried, Alwyn and Thurgot discussed the consequences. Would Malcolm resort to force to evict them and destroy the buildings Kenrick was so painstakingly constructing? The Scottish king, however, did not oppose their presence but asked them to serve him. When they refused, he began to take small disrespectful measures to disrupt their progress.

Bishop Walcher, aware that he had to keep good relations between the Scots and Northumbria was in difficulty. He hoped originally that the monks' settlement would help, but after the exchange of several letters with Thurgot, he grew concerned for their safety and when they refused to return to Durham, he threatened *to excommunicate* Aldwyn and Thurgot *in the presence of the most holy body of Saint Cuthbert unless they should return to him and remain under Saint Cuthbert's protection.*

Sorrowfully, Aldwyn, Thurgot, Kendrick and his trusted carpenter left the monks under the charge of a newly appointed prior. The saintly Scottish queen, Margaret, was deeply disappointed by their departure because she was planning to convert her church at Dunfermline Palace into a monastery and would have welcomed Aldwyn and Thurgot's advice. But she did not forget Thurgot and their paths were destined to cross again.

Upon their return to Durham, early in 1078, Bishop Walcher bestowed on Aldwyn the vill and ruins of Monkwearmouth. On the site, he urged Hailwin to make them *dwellings out of twigs* and at once set about clearing out the church of St Peter, of which only the walls stood in a semi-ruinous state, "but repairable," said Kenrick, with some relief. So, they cut down the trees and cleared the creepers and thorn-bushes that had completely invaded the building.

Once again, a steady flow of postulants arrived, also at nearby

Jarrow and distant Melrose. But the added muscles at Monkwearmouth were a godsend for Kenrick.

Since Thurgot, from the start, had shown a similar calling to spiritual adventure, Prior Aldwyn rewarded him with the monastic habit
of a Benedictine monk and taught him affectionately *how sweet it
was to carry the yoke of Christ.*

The bishop loved these brothers like a benign father and often
visited them, checking on what they lacked and providing generously.
Walcher relied on Aldwyn and Thurgot for advice and they travelled
frequently to Durham to consult with him.

Everything, therefore, seemed to be proceeding splendidly for all
concerned. But, once again, fate had other plans. Christians do not
believe in the weaving of the Norns, but the dreaded sisters were
spinning that of the prince-bishop, Walcher, to his doom.

ELEVEN

DURHAM, NORTHUMBRIA 1078-80 AD

BISHOP WALCHER WAS A SAINTLY MAN, WELL INSTRUCTED IN divine and secular knowledge, but an incompetent leader. He recognised his shortcomings and, so, drew upon advice from trusted men such as Aldwyn and Thurgot. Since these two worthies did not live in Durham, they knew nothing about Walcher's household knights being allowed to plunder and even kill natives without punishment. Also, they did not suspect the undercurrents dividing the bishop's council, for they were not involved directly in these meetings.

The prince-bishop, following the lead of Archbishop Lanfranc at Canterbury, wished to reform the church. In his diocese, this brought him into direct contrast with the Cuthbert community, which enjoyed centuries-old privileges and was now in need of reorganisation. In the city itself, this meant dealing among others with the guardians of Cuthbert's shrine. Walcher's idea was to impose on the *congregatio* the customs of secular canons, to form a community to observe the daytime and night-time offices. For this reason, he was pleased that he now had Benedictine monks like Alwyn within his diocese to serve as an example.

Not everyone agreed with the bishop's plan and the fact that he hired masons and labourers to lay out a central cloister to be surrounded with monastic buildings did not meet with approval among the mighty. In the council, the prelate relied heavily on a local lord named Ligulf, who had fled north after the Conquest. This nobleman was influential also because he had married Ealdgyth, the daughter of the previous earl of Northumbria. While Walcher had high regard for Ligulf and depended on him to represent the Northumbrian lords on his council, the bishop, rather inept politically, did not foresee the trouble brewing with his chaplain, Leobwin. Walcher counted on this cleric and tended to gloss over the frequent clashes between the two men.

Since Walcher incorporated both important secular and religious roles, he could not cope with the administration, so appointed a kinsman, Gilbert, to the role of organising a militia and promoted him as sheriff.

The breaking point came in 1079 when the Scots invaded Northumbria and Walcher was unwilling or unable to deal with it effectively. The invaders, under Malcolm III, were able to plunder Northumbria unopposed for three weeks and return to Scotland laden with booty and slaves. The Northumbrian nobility was outraged and expressed their anger through their mouthpiece, Ligulf.

Leobwin met Gilbert in the newly-constructed cloister, where they would not be overheard. The cleric looked around cautiously, communicating his fear to the officer.

"Gilbert, you have to help the bishop. He is in grave danger!"

This was not true, but the sheriff need not know it.

"How so, what's afoot?"

"Rebellion, my friend. Ligulf oversteps the mark. He refuses to enact our good bishop's reasonable request to make the Cuthbert brotherhood follow canonical rules. How can this be? Many of them are married and subtract sums of money from the Church coffers. It is scandalous! And now," he baldly lied, "they are plotting to murder the earl, our bishop. You must act quickly, my friend!"

"What must I do?" Asked Gilbert, rapidly catching the chaplain's mood. Why should he doubt the word of a man of God?

"Need you ask, Sheriff? Surely, it is clear what you must do. I expect this matter to be resolved before the morrow."

"It will be done."

Gilbert hurried away and summoned men drawn from his available militia; the rest, he gathered from the bishop's armed retinue. He explained the unsavoury task to his captains and referred to the chaplain's admonition that nobody in Ligulf's family should be spared, lest they became the focal point of a subsequent rebellion. They waited till nightfall and then marched swiftly through the town to Ligulf's hall. The two guardsmen at the entrance were overwhelmed and their throats cut. Bursting into the building, they caused servants, with whom they had no quarrel, to scatter in all directions, seeking safety.

Ligulf appeared from an inner room, his face red with outrage, a corded vein pulsing at his neck.

"Sheriff! What is the meaning of this intrusion?"

As if he didn't know! The official's unsheathed blade and those of the men behind him spoke clearly.

Gilbert waved to his subordinates, "Deal with the family!"

"No!" roared the nobleman, staring in horror at the warriors with drawn swords dashing into the room whence he had just come.

It was the last utterance in his life, for Gilbert's sword plunged upwards through the unarmed nobleman's stomach and into his heart. Leaving him lying knees close to his chest, coughing blood and rapidly expiring, Gilbert hastened to observe the massacre in the back room. It sickened him to see the beautiful noblewoman's rich embroidered garb besmirched with gore and the large, attractive eyes staring in horror, without sight, at the roof trusses. Worse were the hacked bodies of two youths who had died nobly trying to defend their mother with nothing more than daggers against the swords and muscles of trained warriors. The younger boy could not have been older than Gilbert's son of two and ten winters. Bile rose in his throat and he had to turn away and return to the body of the hall where his handiwork lay bloodied and motionless.

"For the benefit of his men, he kicked the corpse and spat out,

Traitor! You wished to murder our earl," he looked around at the expectant faces, "but thanks to our excellent work, Bishop Walcher is safe and enjoys good health! Long live the bishop! Long live Earl Walcher!"

This cry was taken up by all the men present and echoed down from the rafters. Servants gazed in horror from behind furniture or drapes.

"You!" Gilbert bellowed at one, "You have witnessed justice enacted in the name of King William. Attend to the bodies and fetch a priest for the funerary rites. See that it is done swiftly!"

Gilbert might have expected Bishop Walcher's gratitude. Instead, the next day, he was summoned by a furious prelate, where he found the chaplain, Leobwin, trembling before him. Walcher turned bulging eyes on the sheriff.

"What have you done?" bellowed the enraged bishop.

"Rid you of a traitor, Your Grace, exactly as the chaplain instructed me."

"Since when has the chaplain given you orders, Sheriff?"

"B-but I understood they were your commands, My Lord."

"They were *not*!" He returned his intimidating stare on Ligulf,

"Idiot! As a result of your deeds and foolish plots, you have destroyed both me, and yourself, and all my family." He waved at Gilbert, a kinsman, to include him in this undoubted tragedy.

Bishop Walcher knew very well that he must placate the unruly Northumbrian noblemen, who had proved a thorn in the side of many kings, let alone a bishop. He dared not remain in Durham, not even within the walls of the castle, where he had established residence. To this end, he sent out a message that he would head a legal enquiry on behalf of the victims' families. To calm the situation, he agreed to meet Ligulf's kinsmen at Gateshead and set out from Durham with a hundred armed retainers because, rightly, he feared for his life. At Gateshead, he met Eadulf Rus the leader of the kinsmen who presented him with a petition of wrongs committed.

The bishop had barely read the date at the head of the document, 18 May 1080, before he cried,

"These are lies and slander! Do not dare to think I will put my signature to this worthless scrap of parchment. Begone!" He screwed up the screed and flung it to the floor.

"You will pay for your arrogance, bishop! Northumbria will tolerate you no longer."

"And who gives you, Eadulf Rus, the right to speak for Northumbria? You answer to King William and, thus, to me by the power vested in me as Earl."

"You are unfit to be earl or bishop and we will replace you!"

Eadulf, enraged, stormed out of the building to organise his men. The bishop, trembling from the release of tension, thought it best to take precautions for his safety and as a man of the cloth, the first thing that came to mind was to seek sanctuary in a nearby church. He did not doubt that Eadulf's threats were heavy with menace, so he called his closest advisers, among them Gilbert and Leobwin.

"Quick! We must flee to the Church of St Mary, it is not far, by the river."

They hastened to the church and Walcher gave orders to his captains to protect the building at all costs. That his orders were being obeyed was clear to the terrified bishop when the clash of arms in the street outside made him clutch at Leobwin's arm. Make haste, see to barring the door!"

This order, too, was obeyed. Soon, the hammering on the stout wooden door indicated that the outnumbered defenders had been overcome, but the massive oak beam resting in its bolted iron brackets could not be breached without the use of an enormous battering ram unavailable to the attackers.

The bishop relaxed enough to kneel before the altar and pray. But St Mary was a church constructed in wood and the assailants brought oil and soaked the doors and walls before setting the place of worship alight. Soon, the greedy flames propagated in the sea breeze and ravaged the edifice.

Inside, Gilbert was the first to notice the smoke curling under the door.

"Fire! They have set the building alight! We must flee!"

"Escape where?" Leobwin sneered, "There is nowhere to flee! *I* am not going out there!"

"Well, I am. I'll take my chance," Gilbert screamed, drawing his sword. "Help me with the bar!" Only the bishop came to his aid. He could not support inevitable death in the flames.

The bar crashed heavily to the floor as they skipped back to save their feet from being crushed. They bent to heave the huge oak beam out of the way so that they could open the doors and rush outside. A raised voice reached the horrified bishop,

"The doors are opening, see beyond the flames! They are trying to escape. Slay them!"

The bishop had a sword with a jewel-encrusted hilt and a gem flashed red in the firelight as he drew it from its calfskin sheath, but the weapon would not protect him. As soon as he found the courage to plunge through the sheet of fire dancing across the doorway, he was hacked by an axe and two swords. He had survived the fire by less than a minute. The angry rebels dragged the body away from the inferno, whilst Gilbert met a similar doom. Greedy hands stripped the bishop of his finery and made off with it until the wretched prelate lay in undignified nakedness in the street.

"Stand back! This is a man of God!" cried a Benedictine monk, covering the bare body with a cloak. It was Aldwyn, who had arrived late for what he had believed would be a public hearing. To his horror, as he approached, he saw the riot and the church in flames. He had begged the mantle from a nobleman who seemed to be an innocent bystander.

"To leave the bishop naked is an abomination in the eyes of God!" he hissed at the lord, who agreed. The donor gazed disdainfully at the bishop's sagging belly and the deep bloody incisions that had ended the bishop's life.

After Aldwyn had covered the prelate he called to two monks standing by the abbey's ox-cart,

"Brothers, come gather up the body, we will take it to the monastery and give the bishop a Christian burial."

From within the church came blood-curdling screams. Stubborn Leobwin refused to face the fury of the mob and chose immolation before the altar where the silver cross was beginning to deform in the heat before his reddened smoke-tormented eyes.

Thus, the reign of the first prince-bishop of Durham ended ignominiously. As the ox plodded slowly away with its gruesome burden, Aldwyn could not help but wonder what would happen to him and his monastery now he had lost the precious support of the man whose remains he was carting sadly away from the scene of his murder.

TWELVE

DURHAM, NORTHUMBRIA 1080-83 AD

Enraged by the death of bishop-prince Walcher, King William reacted in two ways. He sent his Half-brother Bishop Odo to *sort out the Northumbrians once and for all.* The bishop's interpretation was to repeat the harrying of the north, which he did to devastating effect. The king's second reaction was to realise that the concept of a bishop-prince was unsound and so, he appointed a new earl by the name of Aubrey de Courcy.

Odo's horrendous laying waste had an unexpected positive consequence for Durham. King William also nominated a new bishop, William of St Calais, whose response on seeing the ruination of the once-prosperous lands of Saint Cuthbert, was a desire to restore the area to its former glory. Of course, he saw this primarily in terms of the Church. He was dismayed to find that the shrine of such a famous saint was in the hands of married men who were leeching off money from Ecclesiastical coffers in the name of tradition.

Reform! That was the word that spurred him into summoning the worthy Benedictine brothers from Monkwearmouth, immediately after his consecration in January 1081, to express his discontent and expound what he intended to do about it. So, Prior Aldwyn and

Thurgot, his trusted clerk, arrived as commanded, at the bishop's residence within the castle and under the imposing spires of the Saxon cathedral. They found the prelate tense and pacing backwards and forwards.

"It's a disgrace!" the new bishop complained. "This state of affairs can continue no longer! What Durham needs is discipline and devotion—the sort, Brothers, that you have dedicated to Jarrow and Monkwearmouth. I cannot impose this alone, so I mean to write to the Holy Father for support. I'll talk to the archbishop of York and King William. But the reason I called you here today, apart from wishing to meet men of whom, as a fellow Benedictine, I heartily approve, is to reward you with a grant. It is in my power to endow you with the vill of Southwick. The money it generates, I know, will be welcome and spent wisely as you pursue your godly work. The bishop had chosen an important vill near Wearmouth, accessible to the brothers—a splendid and generous gift. This strong, wise, energetic prelate first contacted Thomas, Archbishop of York, who, at the mention of the name Cuthbert, became ecstatic. When he told the archbishop that he intended to found a monastery in Durham to safeguard the shrine, the primate replied,

"Do you know, I was full infirm and look at me today! I spent a night beside the tomb of Saint Cuthbert where I received a vision and the next day, I was completely healed. You have come to the right man, brother in Christ. I shall issue an edict so that you will obtain support for your plan. Meanwhile, I urge you to speak with the king. I feel that you will gain a sympathetic ear because he had an unpleasant experience with the confraternity." He gave William a splenetic smile and added, "I expect he will be glad to see their power reduced."

Prior Aldwyn and Thurgot, engaged with the daily routine of running Monkwearmouth and overseeing Kenrick and his men restore the fabric of the ancient house, were unconcerned by the lack of further news that year. They could not know that their bishop had sailed to Normandy in September to consult with King William.

There, as predicted by the Archbishop of York, he found the king enthusiastic about his idea. It hardly mattered that the king and the bishop's motives were so different. The king regarded Durham as a strategic stronghold—a bulwark against the encroaching Scots. Anything that contributed to consolidating the city met with his favour, quite apart from his long-standing grudge against the *congregatio* of Cuthbert. It was clear that after four hundred years of privileges, this confraternity had degenerated into a body following family traditions, enjoying hereditary prebends. Here, king and bishop met on common ground. The institution was unworthy to continue but, as both men recognised, removing their entrenched power would be no easy matter. King William promised the prelate his unswerving support but suggested that the pope be acquainted with the situation and his approval sought for changes to the *congregatio* and, thus, suitably empowered, William of St Calais returned to Durham.

The bishop summoned all the priests and clerks of the ancient community to Durham cathedral and, gathering them before the shrine of Saint Cuthbert, expounded his decision by concluding,

"The only fitting manner to safeguard the sacred shrine," he waved a hand to indicate the magnificent Saxon tomb, "is to reintroduce the principles to which our beloved saint dedicated his life. Was he not Abbot of Lindisfarne? Did he not lead an exemplary life? The regulation of the Benedictine Order as exemplified by our brothers in Christ at Monkwearmouth, Jarrow and Melrose within this diocese, must for more reason, be introduced around this shrine, here in Durham!" The bishop gazed at the faces surrounding him and felt a surge of discouragement at the unconvinced, sullen countenances that stared back at him. The air prickled with hostility; nonetheless, he continued in a strong, determined voice,

"It is my will and that of King William and our beloved archbishop, Thomas, that we shall found a monastery here in Durham, which will observe the Rules of Saint Benedict. How many of you *clerks*," he sneered as he drawled the word, "are prepared to embrace the vows and become the first monks of Durham Abbey?"

The silence that greeted these words was eloquent—just one clerk stepped forward with hand raised.

The bishop glared around him.

"Know this, my *friends*—for friends we shall remain in the name of our saint and the grace of our Lord. You will not be allowed to stand in the way of progress, however resentful you may feel. I will make a commitment to see that you do not suffer or are not diminished in any wise by the changes." He dismissed them but ordered the lone clerk to stay as they shuffled away muttering and murmuring disgruntled oaths.

"My dear brother," he addressed the wary fellow, "You cannot imagine how pleased I am with you. Will you help me?"

"Ask anything, Your Grace."

William scrutinised his face and there, detected relief, which encouraged him.

"Well then, I need to know the names of the most powerful and hostile of the men who were gathered here. For I must move," he saw the fear and reluctance and altered tone, saying gently, "be not afraid, Brother, I must move to placate them, not to punish them. I was sincere when I said I wished to remain friends."

Convinced, the clerk provided him with four names that the bishop ordered written down despite his notable memory. The prelate, delighted by the man's cooperation asked,

"What are you called, brother?"

"Leofwin, My Lord."

"Splendid, Leofwin, we understand one another. Although the monastery is as yet unfinished, for I must complete the work of my late-lamented predecessor, I appoint you, as of today, chief sacristan of Durham Abbey. Come, I will explain your duties and show you the progress of building that Bishop Walcher began."

The next day, William of St Calais enacted the first stage of his plan, decreeing that churches built in stone would be granted to the four dispossessed clerks whose names Leofwin had furnished. He summoned these men to Durham and could not fail to notice how they arrived with a well-armed retinue. Their fear of the bishop soon dissipated to be replaced with gratitude and joy as he explained his intentions. The first place of worship he selected was the wealthy church of St Andrew at Auckland, which he gave to the most powerful of his opponents. The next, to another overjoyed recipient was St Cuthbert's at Darlington, followed by two churches dedicated to St Mary, one at Easington and the other at Norton. Finally, the bishop ordered the four jubilant men to swear loyalty to himself by kissing his ring. This they did most willingly. In a final act of astuteness, he gave to Eilaf, the former treasurer of the confraternity, the prestigious role of provost at Hexham.

Watching them depart, he turned to his trusted sacristan,

"I do not think, Leofwin, that we shall have any trouble from your old brotherhood. The way is clear for us to create a new order at Durham. I feel sure Saint Cuthbert is looking upon us with great favour."

In his mind, to ensure that was the case, the prelate sent a message to Monkwearmouth asking Prior Aldwyn to present himself in Durham at his earliest convenience. The prior hurried to consult with his trusted acolyte.

"Brother Thurgot, we are to have an audience with Bishop William. What do you think he has in store for us this time? Another endowment?"

"I have no idea, Prior. Am I to come with you?"

"Ay, that is my wish."

Thurgot had a flash of inspiration.

"May I bring Kenrick along with us?"

"If our mason feels he can leave his work for a couple of days. You know how much he cares for his creations."

Thurgot smiled ruefully, having been treated to the rough edge of the mason's tongue on more than one occasion, even though they were the greatest of friends.

"I'll see what he thinks."

Thurgot had reacted on instinct by suggesting that Kenrick

accompany them, but it proved to be an inspiration of historic importance.

When the three men arrived in the bishop's quarters, the prelate was intrigued by the newcomer.

"It is remiss on my part, Master Mason. A little over two years have passed since my consecration and still, I have not come to see your church at Jarrow. They tell me you have done a magnificent job of restoring St Paul's."

"I did my best, Your Grace, with what materials we could scrape together at the time."

"Modesty becomes you, my friend. But I promise I will come to conduct a service within the walls of your church."

"It would be a great honour, My Lord," Prior Aldwyn said.

The bishop had heard but did not comment as all his attention was on Kenrick.

"I hear you worked as a mason in Jumièges, Master Kenrick."

"Ay, I learnt my trade there, Bishop."

The prelate winced but smiled at the discourteous address born of the bluff manners of the rugged builder,

"I had the pleasure of visiting that Abbey last October. I dare say I unwittingly admired some of your work in its magnificent structure. Now, you three will be the first to know that I have spoken with the king about my intention to build a cathedral worthy of Saint Cuthbert's shrine. I want it to be as marvellous as Jumièges if not more splendorous."

Kenrick felt a thrill run through him and he stared at the bishop to gauge whether he was sincere or just indulging a fancy. But he saw the conviction, and it thrilled him even more.

Thurgot glanced at Kenrick and could see the effect of the bishop's words. But then, he, Thurgot had known all along that this was the big man's destiny. He now also understood why he'd had the impulse to invite the mason to this audience: the spirit had moved him. Only Aldwyn of the three attendees was perplexed,

"But Your Grace, there is *already* a cathedral in Durham," he looked pointedly out of the bishop's window at the soaring spires.

The prelate's smile was smug as he turned to Kenrick,

"And we shall pull it down, shall we not, Master Mason?"

If he had been thrilled before, the use of *we* by the bishop left the mason exhilarated.

The bishop wants me to build the new cathedral just like the abbey at Jumièges!

As if in confirmation, Bishop William said,

"Tomorrow, Master Kenrick, we'll meet with Master Askold, he's in charge of the claustral construction and we'll visit the site to hear what you experts have to say."

Kenrick's heart sank. He had just savoured the idea of becoming the master mason in charge of constructing the new cathedral only to have that delightful prospect snatched away almost immediately. This Askold was already building in Durham, surely, he had the advantage. He knew the quarries and the sources of other materials; he would have carpenters and labourers already in his employ. Such were his worries that he completely failed to take in the bishop's next words.

"As for you, Prior Aldwyn, you are to transfer all your monks to Durham. Brother, you are to be the first prior of Durham Abbey. It will be a Benedictine house, run with all the rigour of Monkwearmouth. As soon as the brothers are here, we'll congregate and I shall make all the appropriate announcements. So, return at once to your monastery and make arrangements. You, Master Kenrick, will tell me about your experience at Jumièges..."

The two monks departed in high excitement and chattered on their journey,

"Did you see Kenrick's face when the bishop told us about his plans for a new cathedral?"

"Do you mean before or after he learnt he has a rival."

Thurgot paused and pondered,

"You're right, but there's nobody can compete with Kenrick for skill. Besides, I have known since the day we met that God had plans for him."

"Such as saving your life, Brother, and rebuilding three monasteries? Do you not think they were plans enough for any one man?"

"Nay, Kenrick is destined to greatness, mark my words."

THIRTEEN

DURHAM, NORTHUMBRIA 1085-93 AD

Kenrick studied his rival and, despite not wishing to prejudge anyone, experienced an immediate revulsion for the man. Master Askold's pate was as swarthy as his countenance and well visible because of premature balding, this together with his stocky build and sullen expression gave him an air of menace. In their line of work, involving the need to order carpenters and labourers to briskness, it was most likely an asset. Still, Kenrick couldn't help disliking him on sight.

The bishop had conducted them to the east of the great Saxon cathedral and they stood gazing from the hilltop over the winding river below. William of St Calais, a shrewd judge of humanity, said little, preferring not to influence overmuch the two masons, after all, he intended to hear what *they* could offer. He limited himself to saying,

"It is here that we shall build our new church. It must be the most magnificent in the land to the glory of Saint Cuthbert." No more, no less, issued from his mouth and now his acute eyes studied the reaction of both men. Askold was pacing out steps and counting ostentatiously as he headed downhill eastwards. Kenrick, instead was motionless except for his eyes that moved from the Saxon edifice to the brow of the hill. It was evident that he was pondering.

At last, the sturdy, bow-legged master returned, still counting, to join the prelate and his contender. Kenrick was a deep thinker and taciturn, for he firmly believed that when a man opens his mouth, his words instantly diminish the quality of his thoughts. So, he preferred to remain silent and let Askold speak. For his part, the other mason could not wait to make his announcement. By declaring first, he hoped to display his competence and the right to be master of this prestigious project.

He cleared his throat and with an air of self-importance, said,

"If we are to build the most·magnificent cathedral in the land, it must be six hundred feet long with a nave at least one hundred feet wide. Only then will it compete with the greatest cathedrals in the kingdom, Your Grace." Towards the end of this brief speech, his tone had become wheedling.

Kenrick snorted, causing the bishop to turn sharply and raise an eyebrow.

"Impossible."

Just the one word.

"How so, Master Kenrick?"

"With all due respect to my colleague—"

"Ay, ay, to the point!"

Kenrick's stomach tensed, the bishop didn't suffer fools and this was too important to get wrong."

"The cathedral can be no longer than eighty feet and the nave will have to be, in consequence, narrower than Master A—"

"But I paced it out myself!" cried the offended mason pugnaciously taking one step forward.

The bishop looked appraisingly from one to the other.

"Pray explain yourself better, Master Kenrick."

"Your Grace, if we were to adopt Master Arkold's dimensions, there would be two major drawbacks. First, we would have to demolish the whole of yon cathedral, he waved airily at the Saxon edifice behind them. What then, during construction, would become of the shrine and the church services? You see, there is a natural limit to the east where the land falls away. As it is, we'll have to go deep with the foundations there. With my scheme, we can leave the whole of the west part of the present cathedral standing and open for services and already, the shrine is housed therein."

For Kenrick that was a long speech and, as he feared, he would need to continue because the bishop turned to Askold.

"How do you answer, Master Askold?"

The mason scratched the hair at the nape, where it grew long in contrast to the balding pate.

"He's right, of course, we'll have to knock the lot down, but we can re-use the stone, so that will speed up the work. You want a magnificent church, Your Grace "with his sizing," he sneered, "it'll be too *small*. Anyone can see that!"

He glared triumphantly at Kenrick as if he'd won the argument.

"Well?" the bishop turned to Kenrick.

"It is true that it will be more compact, Bishop," the prelate's eyelids flickered at the lack of grace in the address, "but I will compensate by making it visually more powerful." He tapped a temple with his forefinger, "It's all up here!"

"Ay, easy to say that!" scoffed the other mason, "but where's the proof?"

"At Jarrow."

The prelate surprised him.

"I visited St Paul's two days ago. I was impressed. My compliments, Kenrick. I appoint you as master mason for the new cathedral. Let the project proceed as you say."

"Your Grace, there is one problem. We cannot make any progress until we have built a bridge over the Wear," he pointed upstream, "I mean to quarry over there and as you can see, the land is too steep to bring stone by a direct route to the river bank, so we must cart it along to a place I have identified for the crossing point."

The bishop turned to seek the other mason's point of view, but

Askold was now striding away past the cathedral in a foul mood, regardless of any consequences.

"I fear we have both made an enemy, today, Master Mason. May the merciful Lord bring him to his senses!"

"Amen to that!"

Kenrick had seen the hatred burning in the dark eyes of his rival. He would have to tread carefully because as the master mason, he would have Askold under him and, if all went well, he would become a valuable member of his workforce.

"How long will it take to build the bridge?"

That was a delicate point.

"It depends, Your Grace."

"On what?"

"As ever, on coin and materials"

The bishop, who despite being a monk, had amassed a private fortune, asked,

"Material?"

"Ay, we can build either a wooden or stone bridge, My Lord. I'd prefer stone, say, five or six arches."

"Let it be so. But begin building my cathedral as soon as possible."

They walked away each lost in his thoughts. Kenrick was inwardly jubilant and thinking that there was no reason to delay the excavation of the easternmost foundations. It would be interesting to see how deep his labourers would have to dig to reach the bedrock. At the same time, the bishop was complimenting himself for his selection of a competent master mason. However, it would be a few years before he truly knew what an inspired choice he had made. Thurgot would have said that God had made it, years before.

Within two weeks, Kenrick had his answer—fourteen feet down, the diggers revealed the solid rock he required to start the eastern end foundations. He had pegged out the whole course of what would be the new walls, all the time under the glowers of Master Askold, who went about muttering and cursing anyone who chanced to irritate him further.

Kenrick took a decision. Like the bishop, who came to inspect the site, punctually every morning immediately after Prime, he was impatient for progress. This particular morning, he addressed the prelate circumspectly,

"Begging your pardon, Your Grace, I was wondering...to save time...that is..."

"Ay, spit it out, man!"

"Do I have permission to begin demolishing the east end of the old cathedral."

"Not *so* old, eh?"

The bishop chuckled, for he was not averse to causing displeasure to his Saxon brethren. He had a point, for the *White Church* had been completed just eighty years before.

Kenrick interrupted his thoughts.

"Given that the bridge at Framwell is going to take months if all goes well—and we must allow for the bad weather ahead—well, I thought we could use the stone from yon church to lay the foundations and then begin the walls." When he spoke these words, he had no idea of how optimistic his timescale was. Events would conspire to delay the building of the bridge for years, not months.

"You will not start on the walls until we have had a ceremony but you may proceed with demolition to obtain material for the laying of the foundations."

Progress was, however, impeded by a series of unexpected and unfortunate events. The first occurred in April 1087 when Prior Aldwyn, after a sort illness departed this world, mourned by everyone who knew him. An ashen-faced Thurgot announced the sad news to the chapter,

"Prior Aldwyn was a good and modest man, one of whom the church had a great need for his prudence and counsel, and very conscientious in all things lest he offended God." He stared around at the sorrowful faces of the brothers and felt a sudden desolation. They had been inseparable for years and achieved wonderful things together. For a shameful moment, he felt abandoned and solitary until, thinking of his deceased friend, brought him to the realisation that he was never alone.

The bishop was not in Durham when the prior died because he was engaged in the compilation of a major land survey entrusted to him by King William. His task was to record how many hides of land were in each shire and to whom they belonged. This kept him occupied until its completion in September 1087. So, in practice, Aldwyn had been the abbot in all but name.

Told of Aldwyn's passing, Bishop William, by common counsel of the brothers appointed Thurgot in his place as prior, and ordered him to direct the care of the monastery *within and without.* This meant that Prior Thurgot was responsible for the worship, the finances, the repair of buildings, the discipline, education and spiritual support of the monks. This responsibility extended beyond Durham to the outlying cells spread around Northumbria: Jarrow, Monkwearmouth, Lindisfarne, Farne, Finchale and Crayke. The brothers were gladdened by the appointment but Master Kenrick was overjoyed. Saddened by the loss of his friend Aldwyn, nonetheless, he knew that Thurgot would redouble efforts to build the cathedral, which for the present was stalled.

And yet, there was another major setback and it concerned Bishop William. In his absence, the monastery profited by Thurgot's prudent government. He succeeded in enlarging privileges and increasing the influence of Durham Abbey so that the sacred buildings were improved.

In September 1087, King William died near Rouen and William Rufus claimed the crown of England. Soon after, Bishop William fell out of the king's favour. Many barons rebelled against the new king, favouring Duke Robert, the eldest son of William the Conqueror. The bishop of Durham jeopardised his position by not attending the royal court, which the new king saw as an act of treason, breaking his oath of fealty. The prelate was accused of not supporting the king in resisting the conspirators led by Odo of Bayeux.

The first Thurgot knew of this was when a messenger arrived in Durham in a state of agitation. The barer of the tidings was a Benedictine monk from a southern monastery.

"Prior, my abbot wishes to inform you that Bishop William has been arrested on the charge of treason and all his lands and goods have been confiscated. This was announced at the beginning of March."

Thurgot wondered how this would affect his situation. Would he be left to continue the work he was carrying forward? There was so much to do. News filtered through in June 1088 that the bishop had obtained meetings with the king but without a favourable outcome. In August, he fled to Durham Castle to consider his position. Another messenger came to announce that the bishop's trial would take place at Old Sarum on 2 November. Bishop William summoned his prior, to discuss his plea and, Thurgot, wise and used to royalty from his time with the difficult Olaf in Norway, advised a defence based on canon law.

"Your Grace, your best hope is to refuse to be subject to lay judgement and seek justice from the bishops in canon law."

It was excellent advice but did not allow for the king' turbulent character, who announced,

'You may talk as you please, still you shall not escape out of my hands until you have delivered the castle to me.' Nor did Thurgot take into account the failure of the bishops to support the argument of the bishop of Durham.

The bishop's estates were confiscated on 14 November and on 13 December, to Thurgot's dismay, an army of one hundred knights marched into Durham and took possession of the castle. It was a fearful time for the prior and also for Kenrick, whose work was suspended at such an early stage.

"Have you heard," Thurgot told him, "our bishop has left

England for exile in Normandy. I fear we will suffer many adversities. We must pray at the shrine to Saint Cuthbert."

For once, Kenrick agreed and found himself willingly kneeling beside the prior, imploring the saint,

Please let the king look with favour on the construction of my cathedral.

Their prayers must have been answered, since Thurgot was summoned to the *curia regis* and William Rufus, most humbly, commanded him,

"Prior, in all things attend to the care of the church in complete liberty under yourself as you would have done under the bishop."

Whether it was Saint Cuthbert's intercession, he could not know but instead of harming Durham, the king was kind to them. Differently from his behaviour with other monasteries, he took nothing from them, even giving them money.

Again, unknown to Kenrick, the bishop's absence in Normandy was to work in his favour—not at once, as his impatience would have it—since the bishop was warmly received by the duke, who appointed him to the highest post in his administration. This position he held until 1091, improving relations among the royal brothers. He amassed books for Durham monastery and visited cathedrals and abbeys, making plans for his cathedral in Durham in expectation of his return.

On a journey to the court, Thurgot was involved in one of Cuthbert's miracles. The prior, turned to the two monks accompanying him, wiped the rain from his eyes, and said,

"There's a light over yonder, I think it must be a village, let us seek shelter there in the name of Saint Cuthbert."

They knocked on the door and Thurgot said,

"We are three poor monks from Durham, caught outdoors in this foul weather. In the name of Saint Cuthbert, will you not provide us with shelter and warmth?"

When Thurgot arrived at court, he referred what had happened to the king, continuing,

"We expected the ceorl to give us a kindly reception, instead, he curled his lip and said, 'I don't give a plum stone for your Cuthbert and I'd as soon die as let you into my house', whereupon he at once, collapsed as if dead." The king laughed and beat his hand upon his thigh in great amusement.

"And so, the wretch got what he deserved!" cried William Rufus.

"That's not all, sire!" said Prior Thurgot, "for I called out to our blessed saint not to take the fellow's life and lo! the saint restored him to life before our eyes."

"Did this truly happen?" the king asked awestruck.

"I swear it did, sire."

William Rufus looked around at the other awe-stricken faces and chose his words carefully,

"Nobody can doubt that Cuthbert is among the holiest of men to ever tread the earth of this land of ours as his enduring prodigies continue to prove to us. May Saint Cuthbert intercede for us all!"

Thus, Prior Thurgot had drawn the king's attention squarely onto his saint and city, which he thought could only help their cause.

Whilst construction on the cathedral was suspended, to the joy of Askold alone, Kenrick swallowed his pride and accepted a subordinate role in helping to finish the refectory. The master mason took every opportunity to snipe at and mortify his rival but Kenrick stoically got on with his work and quietly solved problems that Askold's incompetence as an architect engendered. He was wise enough never to vaunt his ingenious solutions, which perversely made Askold hate him all the more.

Thus, it was, that the monks enjoyed their completed refectory with its ingeniously vaulted stone roof, for which Askold falsely claimed the credit, boasting about it to anyone who would listen.

Kenrick confided in his best friend, the prior, as modestly as possible, that the idea was his.

The prior used his influence and freedom in the bishop's absence to continue building the monastic offices for the monks, which was within his remit. But he did not have the authority to begin construction on the cathedral. The claustral work included the undercroft and the south side of the cloister. Outside the dining area, he positioned the *lavatorium* and, therefore, had to provide for water. This meant building a conduit and, all the while, progress had to be made on the important chapter house.

After the completion of construction on the dining hall, a curious episode occurred. One night, the rascally son of the master cook, Rodbert, crept along beside the wall, shuddering at the dark shadows. At last, knowing that he wanted to steal, he spied an open window in the buttery and hauling himself up, wriggled through. Inside, quiet as a stalking cat, he filled a bag with pewter plate and linen, but then made a mistake. Peering round in the dim light, he noticed a faint gleam. Hanging above the prior's table in the dining room was the *schyll*, a bell used by means of a cord to summon the brothers to meals. In reality, it was very old and had more brass in it than tin. Since the monks said it had belonged to Saint Cuthbert, Prior Thurgot ordered it to be splendidly decorated with gold. The young thief, gazing at it, believed wrongly that it was pure gold and tried to detach the bell. His clumsy attempt caused it to ring loudly in the empty room and brought the master cook running and crying,

"Thief! Stop, thief!"

In the gloom, the monk did not recognise his son and delivered a mighty blow to the youth's ear, sending him sprawling and dazed to the floor. In moments, he was surrounded by angry monks, one of whom had had the foresight to bring a candle.

"Why, it's Rodbert!" one exclaimed.

"It's your son, Brother Cook!"

Prior Thurgot came and considered the bag of plates and linen. The bell was still attached and swinging accusingly.

"This is a serious matter, young fellow. To steal from poor monks is an offence to our Lord—you will be punished. Lock him in a strong room for two days without food and drink so that he may reflect on his sins."

Thurgot took the master cook aside and spoke to him in a low voice for a while. The other brothers looked on with concern but, to their relief, saw the cook nod and smile. As usual, Prior Thurgot had dealt with the matter in the best way.

Apart from this singular event, the routine of the abbey continued with the scansion of the services, whilst the lay labourers went on improving the monastic buildings. Kenrick, taken aside by Thurgot, was inconsolable because he could not start building the cathedral. Ill-luck seemed to dog and frustrate him and he told the prior so.

"Do not be ungrateful, Kenrick. Think of Bishop William, condemned to exile. At least, you are here in Durham. Do you not think that the bishop is more irked than you? Instead of complaining, you should go and pray at the shrine of Saint Cuthbert and ask him to bring the bishop back to us."

So, Kenrick did as is old friend suggested and, faith being a mysterious thing, the mason hardly credited the circumstances that followed to his prayers. Malcolm of Scotland invaded Northumbria in May 1091 and reached Chester-le-Street where a small force of men seemed unlikely to stop him but the monks of Durham prayed to Saint Cuthbert for deliverance and, inexplicably, the Scottish king retired in all haste out of fear. Meanwhile, thanks to the good offices of Bishop William, the royal brothers, William Rufus and Duke Robert were reconciled and crossed from Normandy to attack Scotland. For his services, in September, the king restored William of St Calais to his bishopric.

For three days, Edgar the Aetheling, Malcolm's brother by marriage, mediated between Scotland and the Norman brothers while William Rufus was at Durham. Malcom paid homage to Robert not to William Rufus, arguing that he could not serve two masters. Duke Robert returned to Normandy in December. Resentful, the king of England waited for the spring and then took Cumbria for himself, building a castle at Carlisle. He repopulated the area and gave it to the diocese of Durham.

The return of the bishop was in September 1091 and exactly a year later to the month Kenrick received orders to clear the site for the construction of the cathedral. At last! The prelate took Kenrick aside and told him what he had seen at Bernay in France where the mason had decorated the underside of the presbytery arches with *soffit rolls*. Kenrick was fascinated and stored the details in his mind as he was ever open to new ideas. The prelate also referred to the major piers of the nave at Jumièges, alternating with the cylindrical minor ones, which he particularly liked. But, of course, Kenrick already knew about those. Still, he listened to this enthusiasm with pleasure because the bishop's predilections fitted very well with his ideas. Most of all, he was delighted by the clergyman taking him into his confidence.

"Hark, Master, this is what I intend to do. The monks will pay for the monastery building and I will finance the construction of the cathedral. The diocese is much richer than when I was consecrated and can sustain the expense. Shrewd as ever, to expedite his scheme, the bishop granted the rich burgh of Elvet in Durham to the brothers. It contained forty merchants' houses, separate from the bishop's burgh of Durham. So, the monks could trade there, freed from duties payable to the bishop.

Everything seemed to be perfect to proceed with construction but again, the royal brothers argued and the prelate had to return to Normandy to try to settle matters. In June 1093, he returned to Durham, taking Kendrick aside, he said,

"We must arrange a ceremony for the laying of the foundation stones."

FOURTEEN

DURHAM, NORTHUMBRIA, AUGUST 1093-1104 AD

Even Kenrick, who had spent years surrounded by monks, felt the small hairs rise and the skin of his forearms form goosebumps. The brothers had gathered on the building site as dawn was just a hint in the eastern night sky. Kneeling in a wide circle, cowls over their heads, they chanted prayers in unison for the perfect construction of their sacred temple. There was nothing Kenrick desired more but, while he stood succumbing to the eerie atmosphere heightened by the rosy hue cast on the dismembered Saxon cathedral and the stones lying on the ground like extracted teeth, he felt inadequate. Why, he wondered did he find faith so difficult to achieve? Would his life not be more successful and buoyant if he could but emulate the kneeling figures?

His eyes passed over their heads to two men approaching, arms linked, his best friend the prior and his superior, the abbot-bishop, William. Two paces ahead of them strolled two men in splendid garb he had never seen before in his life. One, whose narrow ringlet of gold, tinted pink in the nascent light declared him regal, was Malcolm, King of Scotland. Matching him pace for pace was the new Earl of Northumbria, Robert de Mobray, both come for the ceremony

—what Kenrick had been born for—the inauguration of Durham cathedral. If he had ought to do with it, the new building would be the most splendid church in Christendom.

Kenrick gasped as his gaze strayed above them to the western tower of the old cathedral, now blazing in the glory of the sunrise. He had reprieved this part of the monument from demolition and the adjacent portions of the old church and within lay the saint in whose honour he was about to create the new one. The beauty of the soaring steeple bathed in a delicate pink reminded him of the magnificence to which he should...must, aspire.

Bishop William brought him out of his trance with a crisp, ceremonial speech of welcome to his illustrious visitors. On occasions, and this was one such, simple words contrast with the pomp of the circumstances. Kenrick was grateful for the bishop's swift and efficient presentation because, after waiting for what seemed an eternity, he could not tarry patiently for the ceremony to end and building to begin. The foundations were in place and had been for two weeks. The task of the King of Scotland was to smooth the fresh mortar he had prepared for the laying of the keystone—the corner of the soon-to-rise eastern apse.

The monarch's presence was a political masterstroke, born of Prior Thurgot's correspondence and friendship with the king's saintly wife, Queen Margaret. Bishop William, astute as ever, had realised the opportunity it offered to involve the erstwhile enemy of England in the inauguration. By having Malcolm invest emotionally in the construction, he hoped to deviate any future Scottish hostility away from Durham.

The builders were ready and waiting with the huge cornerstone and Kenrick had laid the mortar in place on the foundations. As if in approval of their purpose, the sun rose in a direct line over the trench to the east and Kenrick solemnly handed the trowel to the king, who pretended for the first and last time in his life to be a mason, smoothing the cement mixture like an expert.

"I declare this building open and may God bless all who work on it and guide their minds and hands," he declared handing the implement back to Kenrick, who had not understood a single word since the king had spoken in Gaelic. The master mason waved to his builders, who swung the great stone, on its wooden hoist so that it hovered over the mortar.

"Down slowly, lads!" he moved two hands, spread-eagled, palms downwards, in a gentle up and down motion. "Stop!" The stone was swinging almost imperceptibly less than one inch above the mortar. "Unbind it!" Two labourers leapt forward and removed the rope, causing the stone to drop the infinitesimal distance onto the mortar. The thick creamy mixture oozed under the enormous weight and Kenrick expertly swiped his trowel around the joint to leave a clean laying. He called for his level and before the onlooking dignitaries, declared himself satisfied, passing his trowel once more for unnecessary scrupulousness and stood back with a huge grin of satisfaction, savouring the historic and most important moment of his life.

Bishop William stepped forward swinging an aspergillum and in a loud voice in Latin, chanted:

Domine Deus, apud quem omne bonum aliquid est suum principium, et per quem illud est melius, et auctus es..." He droned on, leaving Kendrick impatient, so he sidled up to Thurgot and whispered, "What's he saying?"

"...donum pietatis tuae sapientiae. Per ómnia sǽcula sæculórum Amen." ended the prelate.

"Do you want a translation or just a vague idea?" the prior smiled.

"I want to know *exactly*," Kenrick said with a desperate tone that made the prior's grin widen. He understood how his friend regarded the project with the ferocious love of a father.

"The bishop was delivering a blessing, Kenrick, and what he said *exactly* was:

'O God, with whom every good thing has its beginning, and through whom it is improved and increased: grant, we beseech Thee to us who cry to Thee, that this work, which we are beginning for the* *praise of Thy name, may be happily brought to completion through the never-failing gift of Thy fatherly wisdom. Through Christ our Lord Amen.'*

The prior laid an amiable hand on his dear friend's arm, "Happy now?" he grinned up into the tall mason's ecstatic face. He, Thurgot, had known in his soul that this day would come and he was over-joyed, too.

"I hope his blessing works," Kenrick, ever the bluff speaker, growled. But he knew deep inside that it would. He would show everyone, kings, bishops, priors and monks, what Kenrick, descendant of the man who had befriended the saint in the shrine, was capable of. If Saint Cuthbert was kind enough to guide him, so much the better! Let work begin! He began roaring orders as the important visitors carefully picked their way over the rubble and wood littering the site.

One day, great lords will have difficulty obtaining finery worthy of this place.

Thought Kenrick.

By the time the bell in the Saxon tower chimed for Sext, the entire first course was laid; when it pealed for Vespers, the second was done and only the fading light persuaded Kenrick to call a halt. At this rate, he mused, the walls of the apses up to roof height would be complete within the first month.

Master Mason Kenrick was not alone in fulfilling his destiny. Bishop William summoned Prior Thurgot to his quarters before the day ended.

"Prior, I have come to a perhaps overdue decision. Throughout my enforced absences since..." his brow creased and he calculated, "...since 1088, you have been unofficially my reliable and most worthy deputy. It is time to formalise your role."

He explained his intention to the satisfied monk and the next day, led him before the people of the whole bishopric and enjoined him to be his representative over them as archdeacon.

"You, Prior Thurgot, henceforward to be known as *Archdeacon*

Thurgot, will exercise pastoral care over this, your flock, throughout the bishopric and whoever might succeed you as prior shall similarly assume the office of archdeacon."

This decision meant that Thurgot was given special powers and privileges. He could preside over synods in the absence of the bishop and was to be his deputy as abbot.

As he walked away from the gathering, Thurgot's mind was racing, trying to come to terms with what he could now achieve. Uppermost among these was the certainty that with the see embracing Cumbria, East Lothian, and Hexhamshire, he would have the finances to shower Kenrick with all the money needed to expedite the building of *their* cathedral. All he required was for the bishop to absent himself from Durham. If precedent meant anything, that was an almost foregone circumstance.

Meanwhile, Kenrick, returned to his lodgings, had a surprise. Yowling at his door was a ginger kitten with absurdly large yellow eyes staring up at him. The mason, who led the solitary existence of a half-monk, half-builder, had no companion in his life.

WHY NOT? But I'll have to make some arrangements.

The kitten was playful and affectionate and Kenrick, having given it a bowl of milk, picked up the waif and discovered that it was ot just milk that the little creature lapped up but also his caresses. The relationship was off to an excellent start but there was still the problem of what to do about the cat whilst he was at work.

The little wretch will need company, it'll be bored otherwise.

He solved the problem by offering a silver coin to the woman who took in his washing. One silver coin a week was worth paying for having the company of the adorable feline.

The following spring of 1094 brought a royal writ ordering *'William, son of Thierry and all the king's lieges of Carlisle and all who abide beyond the Lowther to accept spiritual jurisdiction of the bishop and archdeacon of Durham.'*

This was the authority Thurgot needed over the most turbulent and uncooperative part of the diocese. Henceforward, he hoped, his administration would be plain sailing and whenever he visited Kenrick's rapidly-growing edifice, his heart swelled with optimism.

An opportunity arose at once for him to exert the authority of the bishopric. On discovering that Eadulf Rus had died murdered by a woman— the selfsame nobleman who had led the mob to slaughter his friend, Bishop Walcher— he reacted immediately. With a clamorous proclamation, he ordered the body exhumed and the corpse thrown by the wayside for the carrion to feed on. It was a test of his authority over the querulous lords, none of whom dared to challenge his decision.

Next, he recognised the importance of seeking the patronage of the Scottish king for peace and unity with England. Knowing that Malcolm and his queen, Margaret, would wish to confirm blessings from the community of Saint Cuthbert and aware that the queen was terminally ill, he sought to solemnise a bond of confraternity. This was to be between the Scottish royal house and the Durham community. The area of Cumbria, part of the Durham diocese, was still contentious between Scotland and England, so, in August, Malcolm travelled to the royal court at Gloucester to resolve the problem. There, he was informed that his plea had to go before the *curia regis* and the judgement of the barons. Malcolm replied that he would not settle the border issues without the presence of the Scottish barons. The two kings never met.

Meanwhile, Bishop William once again fell into disfavour with King William Rufus in a dispute over the archbishop of Canterbury's relations with Pope Urban. The king refused to recognise this pope and so strained became the relations between the king and the bishop of Durham that it marked the end of the prelate's public career. He performed his last episcopal duty in Northumbria with his archdeacon on 29 August 1095 in the cemetery of Norham on the confines with Scotland, when the gift of lands in Lothian to Saint

Cuthbert by Malcolm and Margaret was confirmed by their son, Edgar.

In January occurred an event of considerable significance for Archdeacon Thurgot. A conspiracy against the king led by some nobles brought about the arrest of the earl of Northumbria. Tainted by association, Bishop William was ordered to appear at the Christmas court, but, stressed, he fell ill on arrival. He received the last sacraments on 1 January 1096 and died the next day. His body was borne on a litter from Windsor to Durham drawn by horses. The journey took a fortnight. On his deathbed, Bishop William declared that his corruptible body *'should in no wise be laid in the same building as the incorrupt body of Saint Cuthbert'*. Thurgot ordered a solemn ceremony for the man he had grown to admire and respect, ordering a burial in the chapter house, beside Bishop Walcher. The bishop was laid to rest in a gold-embroidered robe ornamented with griffins. The brethren of Durham Abbey grieved at his death and some worried about a possible successor. But King William was in no hurry and Thurgot safeguarded the lands and customs of the bishopric whilst there was no incumbent aided by a royal writ instructing the king's sheriff and vassals of Carlisle to obey Thurgot, the archdeacon of Durham "in matters spiritual as they did in the time of William bishop of Durham."

Still, the bishopric remained vacant until 1099 since the king enjoyed an income of £300 a year from the see. This diverted sum brought spending on the new cathedral to a halt but Kenrick had raised the walls so that an uncovered shell graced the site. When Thurgot, somewhat worried at the financial situation, entered the partial edifice, Kenrick proudly showed him the completed transepts, choir piers and wall arcading. The choir piers and walls reached up to the height of his proposed aisle vaults.

"No wooden roof for us, Archdeacon, I'm pondering a solution using stone."

"But the money—" Turgot cut short his objection at the sight of his friend's distressed expression, adding, "God will provide."

Whether Kenrick believed the archdeacon or not, he decided to test his revolutionary scheme to create a stone vault over the choir aisles. Spurred on by the scorn of Master Askold who taunted him that only a wooden roof could be achieved given the weight of stone needed, Kenrick was determined to prove him wrong. To do so, he had to invent something never before built in the world. When the new bishop arrived in 1099, he found the choir constructed up to the window sills but the aisles covered with the spectacular rib vaulting.

King William Rufus decided to forgo the income from the Durham see in 1099 in exchange for £1000 paid by Ranulf Flambard, his agent, who had a private fortune. He was consecrated on 5 June and one of his first acts was to visit the site of the new cathedral and demand to see the master mason. Kenrick arrived and bent to kiss the ring of office while the bishop gazed in admiration around him, finding the cathedral all but completed. The nave was unfinished, but the choir, transepts and crossing and much of the nave to help support the crossing were in place.

Flambard, an intelligent and informed man as well as being ambitious, immediately spotted the rib-vaulting and catching Kenrick's arm, said, pointing to the ceiling,

"Explain this!"

Proud of his achievement and glad to elaborate to someone who had some inkling of what he had attained, he began,

"There were many doubters, Your Grace. They said a stone vault could not be built. So, I got to thinking and the problem was the weight of the stone. It came to me in a flash...I had to build ribs that would serve two purposes, take the weight but create a pleasing effect for the eye—"

"Which, praise the Lord, you did!"

"Ay, see how the ribs seem to grow effortlessly upwards and the vigorous slender lines of action— just as I imagined them in my head —make you forget the massive surfaces between."

"It is magnificent! But tell me the details of how it was done."

Kenrick was only too happy to oblige after he had bellowed

orders to three men raising a large stone in the nave. He spoke for many minutes, delighted that the prelate's concentration never once wavered. He could gauge his interest from his eyes.

"...so, we built the transverse arches and the ribs separately on their own centring, filling the cells with less substantial masonry. That was the knack, My Lord. Up here, in the western bay, you're looking at a thickness of between a foot and sixteen inches." The mason saw that he could risk further detail as the bishop seemed enchanted in a way that not even his friend, Thurgot, could match. He indicated upwards, "See, the cells are built of coursed rubble, with stones of about eighteen inches long, though it varies slightly, on the soffit they are about two and a half inches thick...but..." his finger moved downwards, "...at the lower part of the cells they are about four inches thick. We used oak boards..." he droned on at length until the prelate asked about quarrying and Kenrick led him outside to gaze across the river, where, by chance, a team of horses was pulling a cart laden with stone down the hillside track.

More than satisfied, Bishop Ranulf turned to the mason,

"Master, we shall finish the cathedral together, your genius and my money," he chortled and clapped the older man on the back.

Kenrick beamed into the face of the suave Frenchman and bluff as ever, growled,

"Ay, that we will, Bishop."

For a while, the bishop was able to make good on his promises but disaster was to strike him and the cathedral building. In August of the new century, William Rufus died when shot by an arrow while out hunting. It was accepted as an accident, but voices circulated even as far as Durham that it was an assassination. Some accused a man called Walter Tirel, who they said was acting under orders from William's younger brother, Henry, who promptly seized the throne. The new king, Henry I had a great thirst for money and on a false charge had Bishop Ranulf arrested and imprisoned but the wily, rich bishop escaped and fled to Normandy.

Once more, Thurgot was left in charge of the diocese with all the duties it implied. Between preaching, consecrating new churches and investing priests, the archdeacon this time had to deal with the demands of the king's new agent who came to claim the revenue from the bishop's estates.

To make matters worse, the unscrupulous king took over estates legitimately owned by the diocese. Estates were also misappropriated by the vengeful king and diverted to other dioceses. Thurgot had to choose.

"Don't worry Kenrick, I will give you the money you need to continue."

This he did, but at the expense of the monks whose buildings he neglected. In Flambard's absence, Kenrick finished the eastern arm of the cathedral, the eastern transept and the crossing by 1104. The master mason was ageing. His one desire was to see his masterpiece completed before he left this world. He had reached his sixty-fifth winter by 1104 and his aching joints no longer allowed him to mount the scaffolding with his former agility—something his bitterest enemy had noted with an unpleasant curl of his dust-encrusted upper lip.

FIFTEEN

DURHAM, NORTHUMBRIA, 1104 AD

A FOUL-MOUTHED CURSE ECHOED IN THE EERIE DARKNESS OF the night-time cathedral illuminated only by the moon and a solitary taper in the hand of the blasphemer. He had stubbed his toe against a stone lying in the under-construction nave. The intruder whispered to himself,

"Loudmouthed fool! You'll give yourself away if you go on like that!"

Learning from experience, he kept his eyes on the ground and avoided further pain to his feet or worse, tripping and causing himself a serious injury. Anyway, he did not have far to walk, the wooden scaffolding rose above him, where the labourers were raising stone for the new northern wall.

Tilting his candle carefully so that the molten wax fell on a flat rock, he quickly worked the taper into the pool of wax before it set, thus fixing it upright. He looked up at the scaffolding and grunted, aware of the dangers involved. The light was insufficient for the hazardous climb but needs must. If his plan was to work, it had to be executed at night. So, nerves steeled, a muscular arm stretched up and the man heaved himself onto the wooden frame, finding a foothold and pushing forward to the first platform, but he had no interest in stopping there—not high enough. On he went, slowly, not confidently, as he would have climbed in daylight until he reached the underside of the top platform.

The delicate part of the operation was here, where he wished to tamper with the fastenings but at the same time, not make it obvious to anyone arriving from below. He wanted to create an invisible death-trap, so he reached into his belt and drew out a sharp knife from its leather scabbard. The blade gleamed dully in the weak moonlight, but what he could not see, he could manage by touch. Patiently, he set about his task because there was no hurry. He calculated that nobody was about at this time of night and even if by some diabolical chance somebody passed by the building, the chances were that they would not even notice the solitary dim flame flickering below. Time was on his side. Even so, the rope was tough, it had to be to do its job and his expert hand felt the binding, eliciting a grunt of approval at the competence of the man who had performed the knotting. But right next to and behind the knots, he began to saw at the unyielding hemp, swearing under his breath at the rigid rope. Slowly, he proceeded, haste might lead him to saw through the last strands and that would defeat his purpose—just so far through and no more—he paused and felt with his fingernail. Ay, that was about it. He did not risk sawing any farther into the rope but turned and reached up to the outer edge of the platform. He had preferred to work next to the wall until he got the feel of what he was doing. Here on the outside he risked becoming the victim himself and that was decidedly not the plan. In the dark, heart thumping, he held his breath as he inched his foot towards the edge of the platform, conscious all the while of the drop of over seventy feet to the ground below.

"High enough to break a man's neck!" he breathed gleefully, sucking in the air his cautious advance had denied his lungs. Reaching up to the knotting, he repeated the previous operation until the rope was almost sawn through. That done, he paused and considered. Was there any need to saw the other side of the platform, too?

His practical knowledge told him that it was unnecessary and, also, the more he cut, he thought craftily, the more chance of his tampering being seen: to be avoided at all costs. So, he replaced his knife in its sheath and climbed down to the ground—never in his long career had he descended scaffolding so slowly, but he did not want to risk ruining everything now by hurting himself and being found injured and compromised.

His cunning was such that when he detached the candle, he remembered to scrape away all traces of wax from the stone where it had stood. There must not be the slightest evidence of his nocturnal presence to raise suspicion.

The question he had to consider was whether to return to his soft bed or to curl up here on the uncomfortable ground. He weighed up the pros and cons. On the one hand, he wanted to be the first to arrive in the morning. What morning! The dawn was only a matter of two hours away. On the other, he feared oversleeping because he had deprived himself of rest—willingly—he sniggered. But what if the first arrival found him slumbering here with a candle stub beside him? That would never do! The issue decided, he sneaked away and reached his lodgings unseen.

His feverish thoughts, full of *what-ifs*, prevented him from dozing, so, at best half-asleep, he did not fail to hear the first cock crow and see the faint light of dawn. Leaping up, he threw cold water in his face and hurried outdoors in the clothes he had not removed the evening before or on his return that night.

It was no surprise therefore that he was first on the site and watched the labourers begin their usual tasks. What he needed to do was to prevent any of them from climbing the scaffolding. No, that honour was reserved for only one person, the accursed master mason — and serve him bloody well right, the big-headed upstart! Ha! Here he was approaching. Worries over, Askold turned to Kenrick and began his act.

"Last night, on inspection, I could have sworn that the last course was placed askew. I didn't say anything at the time because everyone was exhausted and ready to leave." He gazed upwards, fully aware that the scaffolding platforms impeded any consideration of the masonry.

"Well, up you go! You'd better check whether your impression was right."

Kenrick handed the mason his own straight-edge plumb. But he noticed the hesitation and strange look in the man's close-set eyes. It rang an alert.

"Go on, then!" he growled.

"Not I, this needs the *expert* eye of the master mason unless you're *too old* to do the job," his words dripped with sarcasm and provocation.

Kenrick snatched back his straight-edge and slid it into the wide pocket of his leather apron. He reached up with one hand to the scaffolding but he had not detached his gaze from the sturdy mason. There was no doubting that gleam of satisfaction in the man's eyes as his huge hand closed on the wooden frame.

He's up to no good, that's for sure!

He paused and instead of pulling himself up, he said,

"Maybe you're right, Askold, and I am too doddery to scale this scaffolding. I order *you* to go up."

This command was well within his rights as the master mason.

"Me? I ain't going up there!"

Everyone saw the terror in the mason's face.

"Eggert! Bertram! Seize him and hold him tight! Faruin," he called to a strapping labourer whose honest hard work had attracted his attention and caused him to learn the youth's name, "Get you up there! Do not climb up to the last platform but inspect its bindings."

At these words, there were angry murmurings among the small crowd of builders that had gathered around the pinioned captive. Each man knew the dangers of climbing scaffolding so high from the ground. One false grip, easy enough with tools in your hand, meant disaster. The thought that a scoundrel might deliberately make the frame unsafe made them seethe with fury.

All eyes were turned upwards watching Faruin's progress except for Askold's that were fixed on the ground. They watched the youngster move on the penultimate platform and poke about the binding on the left. Then he moved to the right and repeated the inspection but this time, he took a long time about it. At last, he knelt to seek his foothold and begin the descent.

When he was back on the ground, everyone was holding his breath and straining to hear the youth speak, he turned to Kenrick and his words came panting from exertion,

"You were right, Master. The bastard's sawn through the ropes on this side," he pointed upwards. "It'd only need a man's weight an—"

There was no time for him to finish before Kenrick's huge fist smashed with all the force he could muster into the mason's face. The crack and the blood told the tale of a broken nose. And a collective growl of satisfaction bode ill for Askold.

But, other than this punch, Kenrick would have no rough justice served on *his* cathedral site. He turned back to Faruin,

"Lad, are you quite sure of what you saw?"

"Certain, Master, I swear the ropes are held by nought but a strand."

"Well then Faruin, run now to the castle and fetch the sheriff and his men." Turning to another mason, he said, "Talking about rope, Master Ganhart, bind this ruffian good and tight... his legs too. We don't want him running off, do we?"

"I ain't done nothing! You can't prove a thing!"

"In that case, you won't mind proving your innocence by climbing to the top, will you?"

The look of panic returned, followed by cunning consideration. He was likely wondering whether he could climb up on the left and not make the platform collapse. But as well as being a rogue, he was a coward.

"I told you! I ain't going up there!"

"Well, that's as good as a confession, lads! Bind him!"

The sheriff, a stolid Norman knight, arrived with six burly men at his back.

"Master Mason," everyone in the town knew who Kenrick was, "this youth has some garbled tale about attempted murder."

"You can prove nought!" Askold growled.

"Silence! You'll have your turn to talk. Master Mason?"

Kenrick explained all the events calmly as well as stressing the two refusals of Askold to climb the scaffolding."

"Why are his face and beard bloodied."

Kenrick did not hesitate.

"When I realised he planned to have me fall from the top," he pointed at the impressive height, "I lost my temper and hit him. He wanted to kill me."

"You did well, Master, well within your rights." The Norman sneered at the cowering prisoner, "You wanted to take his job, did you? Well, we'll see. You and you, get up there and check out what the youth says is true. If it is, you'll face a just punishment. Attempted murder is a serious offence. Envious of the better man, were you?"

"I ain't saying nothing!"

"Have a care, you two!" the sheriff called up.

The crime confirmed, the builders and masons hissed at Askold and some hurled insults far from fitting for a sacred building.

"Lucky your cathedral hasn't been consecrated, Master Kenrick, I'd have to arrest half your workforce for desecration. As it is, you'll lose this one—one way or the other," he added ominously.

As the sheriff and his men led the miscreant away, another mason clapped Kenrick on the back,

"You did well to avoid a tragedy, Master. That rogue was always whispering about you, trying to belittle and besmirch your reputation but nobody paid him any attention we all know you're ten times his worth as a mason."

"I'll be worth nought if I don't get yon scaffolding secured. Take a rope and sort it out, lads! Oh, and," he had an afterthought, "whilst you're at it, check the course is level. You never know."

In reality, Kenrick had strolled into his cathedral with other things on his mind. He had grown up with the Saxon custom of decorating flat surfaces and whereas he did not wish to utilise old-fashioned ideas on his church, neither did he want to abandon what he considered to be an estimable tradition. So, whilst his workers were scurrying about their various tasks, everyone grateful that nothing grave had happened to their beloved master and each wishing to impress him with their commitment to his cause, he strolled around the exterior of the building and studied the excellent but unadorned stonework at ground level upwards.

Once, while he was in Normandy, he had visited the church of St Étienne in Caen and he remembered the arcading in the apse that he had admired. Ay, something like that was needed, but more expressive. He would make notes before he forgot. A sketch might be useful. He was lost in these thoughts when a familiar voice called to him.

The archdeacon was advancing with a determined stride,

"Is it true, Kenrick?"

"What?"

"They're all saying there was an attempt on your life."

"Ay, Master Askold did try to get rid of me."

The cleric stood frowning, his countenance revealing a series of emotions, after searching his mind for an appropriate citation, he quoted from Proverbs,

"A heart at peace gives life to the body, but envy rots the bones."

"What? Oh, ay, some of the lads were saying that he was envious—"

"Envy is a mortal sin, Kenrick."

"I don't know about that, I always treated Askold fairly."

Thurgot smiled fondly at his old friend,

"It's not really about you, Kenrick. It was his head. It never did cope with you becoming master mason in his stead. Think about how many years it was festering before he acted. The man's a coward and nowhere near as good a mason as you. The Normans will hang him, you know."

"I don't want that. He's still a good mason."

Again, the fond smile but it was followed by an angry flash,

"Reflect before you speak, Master, God commands *thou shalt not kill* but that scoundrel wanted to break your neck."

"I suppose. You priests are always right."

"Except I'm a monk, not a priest."

"Same bloody thing!"

Thurgot snorted and clapped Kenrick on the back, somewhat harder than mere affection. He turned to stride away unable to linger with all the responsibilities he shouldered in the absence of the bishop.

Kenrick watched him go and chuckled with satisfaction, he had reiterated his declared attitude to holy men, but he had a lot of time for Thurgot. He was different, the fact that he could say what he thought to his face and the monk never bore a grudge proved it and spoke volumes for their friendship. Very soon, though, he'd give the archdeacon a friendly pat on the back and see whether he stayed on his feet!

The thought of the power in his arms snapped him into action. He hastened back inside the building—he'd show them all whether he was past his prime!

A few of the labourers raised curious heads to stare as, defying his age, he hurried straight to the scaffolding and flung himself upwards, straining muscles to move skywards like a giant spider in its web. Such haste was a bad example and extremely hazardous. The men below knew it and only the dimmest among them did not understand that the master was making a statement. Each of them breathed easier as he clambered up to the now secure upper platform and, from down there, they could hear his booming voice encouraging his masons as they positioned another course of stones along the almost completed northern external wall. They exchanged looks and grins—the world of the cathedral had returned to normal.

SIXTEEN

DURHAM, NORTHUMBRIA, AUGUST 1104

S*HAPED RATHER LIKE A QUINCE,* THOUGHT ARCHDEACON Thurgot as he admired the cooking apples ready for picking in the monks' orchard of Durham Abbey.

"These are unusual apples, Brother," he said, pointing to a tree laden with the green fruit, and turning to his guide, the monk in charge of the abbey gardens, "what name do they go by?"

"Dog's Snout, Archdeacon. I believe this variety was so called because of its shape," he picked one of the curious apples and handed it to his superior, "see how it tapers similar to a hound's nose? They are rather acidic, so the master cook uses them to bake pies. You'd be wise to avoid sampling it."

Thurgot had more weighty matters to deal with and it was to distract himself that he had chosen to tour the gardens. He did not need to keep the gardeners on their toes because their efforts with fruit and herbs kept the cooks well stocked with essential seasonal produce. He handed back the dog's snout and excused himself, saying he had pressing matters to attend to, which was, if anything, an understatement. The eastern end of the new cathedral was complete and ready to receive its saint—well, almost. Kenrick had done a magnificent job. If the prior had to be honest, and although he had always had an instinctive faith in his friend, in his wildest imaginings, he would never have dreamt that the mason was so capable. It was no exaggeration to say that he was blessed with the talent of a genius. It confirmed Thurgot's long-standing theory that God had driven Kenrick to save him from the turbulent devouring sea all those years ago so that he, in turn, might entrust the construction to the Saxon.

*How ironic, it's a Saxon building this **Norman** cathedral!*

Whatever the case, Kenrick had provided a home for the saint. Now it was his turn, in the absence of the bishop. That entailed chasing up his orders of wood-carvings, choir-stalls, chandeliers, candelabra and the altar furnishings, in other words, all the embellishments necessary to make Saint Cuthbert's house his home. The church would have to be ready for the end of August since he had established the 29th as the ceremony for the translation of the saint's body. He had invited the nobility and clergy of Northumbria, and beyond, and one or two had begun to arrive early. The bishop had promised to come from Normandy and that was made possible by his restitution and absolution following reconciliation with King Henry. The prelate had started to retrieve his estates from those occupying them and that would mean more money for Kenrick to finish the nave and the other remaining work, towards completion.

As the days sped past, Thurgot grew nervous, for everything had to be perfect. Some of the more dilatory craftsmen would have to be chastised and he could only do that effectively in person. Thurgot spent the week before the ceremony successfully getting everything consigned into the eastern arm of the cathedral and had to admit that his diligence and the various skills of the artisans involved, honoured the masterpiece of a cathedral housing their work. Just when he thought he could relax, something regrettable troubled him. As the guests began arriving, there was increasing murmuring about the claims of the monks regarding the legend of Saint Cuthbert, including the incorruption of the body.

The head sacristan came to him distressed,

"Leofwin, I can see you are in a state. You'd better tell me what's upsetting you so."

The monk's face crumpled and Thurgot feared he was about to weep but he gathered himself and in a broken voice, said,

"Archdeacon, a group of brothers came to me with the same tale. Voices are circulating that the incorrupt state of Saint Cuthbert's body is nothing more than the faith of tradition, kept alive by us monks for profit."

Thurgot's face grew puce with rage and frustration and, before he could react, the sacristan added,

"They say it's impossible that the passage of four centuries would allow the body to remain in the same state as before the time of Bede."

Thurgot tried to speak but only a low growl issued from his throat.

Brother Leofwin took it as a sign that he could continue, so he did,

"I heard one nobleman say he wondered whether we even had possession of the saint's ashes, I ask you! What sort of unbeliever have we invited to our cathedral?" he looked anxiously at the archdeacon who seemed to be unwell, "what are we to do, Your Grace?"

The use of such an elevated title brought Thurgot back to himself.

"We must do several things, foremost among them is to pray for guidance; secondly, we must summon our brethren to a meeting in the chapter house to discuss the matter and finally, dear Leofwin, we must pray to our saint. He might well give us a sign."

The archdeacon called the assembly for the 27th and that night the strangest event occurred. It was an occurrence that had a determining impact on the deliberations of the following day in the chapter house; also, it was an episode that the prior interpreted as the sign invoked. Kenrick had not succumbed to Thurgot and the monks' pressure to remove the timber centring supporting the vault of the presbytery. Since the internal width of the apse was thirty-one feet, Kenrick had decided to wait until the last minute.

The first Thurgot knew about the removal was when the furious Kenrick, bristling, accused him and his monks of having removed the timber.

"You are a pack of irresponsible idiots!"

"Watch your tongue, my friend. I have no idea what you are talking about! None of the monks, to my knowledge, has laid a hand on your blessed supports."

"Well, they are gone! Someone took them in the night and risked bringing down the whole vaulting. My men are adamant that they didn't do it so that only leaves your lot!"

The archdeacon had a faraway look in his eye and suddenly it was replaced with a beatific smile.

"Kenrick, my friend, you know what we have here, don't you?"

"Haven't a clue."

"None of your men and none of the monks did it, so it's clear, isn't it?"

"Are you deliberately talking in riddles?"

The monk beamed at his friend,

"It's obvious, it was *him*!"

"Who? Damn it, Thurgot! Who?"

The archdeacon rebuked him,

"You must mind your language when we are discussing certain matters."

"What bloo—blessed matters?"

Thurgot grasped his friend's arm and squeezed, his face alight with divine bliss,

"It was Cuthbert! The saint removed the timbers himself. That's why there was no damage. It's a sign, Kenrick. The holy man wants his home to be perfect, don't you see."

"Ay, well, he could have waited, I was going to take it down myself the day after tomorrow. It looks like my vaulting's good and solid anyway."

"Humph! Always the same old Kenrick! Even in the face of a miracle, all you can conceive of is masonry."

"Lucky for you that's what I think about; else you wouldn't have a place to bung your saint."

"Kenrick! You're incorrigible," he said to the mason's broad back as, not dismissed, the master walked away. "But I can't help but love you," he murmured, too low to be heard.

To the astonishment of the gathered monks, the archdeacon recounted the miracle of the timber supports. Some of the brothers crossed themselves, others fell to their knees and cried words of praise. No one for a moment doubted that it was a sign. Once the euphoria had passed, the tension returned because everyone was alarmed at the rumours circulating, especially with the bishop's imminent arrival.

As the spokesman of the community, the sacristan, Leofwin took the floor.

"Your Grace," he addressed the archdeacon with the title reserved to the bishop, "I fear it will take more than this miracle to convince the doubters. After all, we have no concrete proof in this case." He added inaudibly, "Excuse the pun," raised his voice and said in ringing tones, "we must open the sarcophagus."

Thurgot looked appalled for a moment, reflected and said, "That is something our bishop must decide. He will be here on the morrow."

A lone voice at the back of the chapter house was heard to say, amid hushing, "More's the pity!"

Thurgot knew that he was popular among the brothers and his administration was widely admired, so he smiled thinly at the comment and decided to treat the brethren to an uplifting tale.

"When I was in Norway, many years ago," he paused with a faraway expression on his face and his audience was rapt, "King Magnus, we called him *the Good,* ay, and he was..." Again, the distant look came to his countenance, "...he was the son of Saint Olav and every year, just once, opened his father's tomb to trim his beard and cut his nails." He watched their awed reactions and heard the murmuring, and after a moment's pause raised his hand so they all fell silent, "Brothers! No one is entitled to compare the holiness of saints but I say, with the confidence of King Magnus the Good, we can safely open the tomb of our Saint Cuthbert if only Bishop Ranulf permits us."

The meeting dispersed with the monks, as Thurgot had foreseen and hoped, in a less anxious and ashamed state. But his good work was undone by the arrival of Bishop Ranulf Flambard, who, to the archdeacon's dismay, united his voice to the sceptics.

"Surely, Thurgot, you wouldn't have me believe that after four hundred years, plus the vicissitudes of the journeys following the Viking raids and the negligence of the attendants that the saint is entire." His features had an arrogance that Thurgot had never appreciated but now he wished to slap the surly superiority from his face. His vows, gentleness and respect for his position quelled such thoughts but he could not conceal what was hidden behind his visage.

"Come, come! Surely you do not wish for my authorisation to open the tomb?"

"Your Grace, what do we have to lose? If you are right and there are only bones, it will confirm the doubters. But if not, the see will gain enormously in prestige." He went on to relate the miracle of the previous night and with unshakable faith insisted it was a sign to proceed.

In the face of such devotion from his immediate subordinate, Ranulf could no longer hesitate.

"Very well, this is what *you* will do."

His instructions were crisp and concise, also because he was in a hurry to encounter some members of the nobility to discuss the return of lands to their rightful owner—himself.

Obeying his orders, Thurgot summoned his sub-prior, happily named Aldwine, Leofwin the chief sacristan, Brothers Algar, Wilkin, Osbern, Godwin and the other sacristans Henry and

William and Symeon, who was to chronicle the event, in all, a total of nine monks.

On 24 August 1004, as soon as their brethren had retired, Thurgot and the brothers he'd selected fasted and prayed. Afterwards, they prostrated themselves before the venerable coffin and some of them tearful with emotion laid hands upon it. In the atmospheric candlelight, with trembling hands, using iron tools, awed and fearful, they began to force open the lid. They quickly succeeded and to their astonishment, inside found a metal-bound chest covered on all sides with hides and fixed to it by nails.

"Pssst!" Thurgot regained control over their fears, "Brothers, the Lord is with us, overcome your terror and set about the task of opening this chest. In a matter of seconds, the iron bands were forced open and the lid raised. Within lay a wooden coffin, covered by a coarse linen cloth, the length of a man. The material, they tested with trembling fingers and agreed that it had been impregnated with wax. Leofwin encouraged them to remove the cloth and laid it reverently aside.

"Come," said the sacristan, Raise the coffin, we'll move it from behind this altar, into the middle of the choir, where we can better investigate."

"Excellent thought, Brother, Thurgot commended him, "it is more spacious and more suited to our purpose."

They took away the lid of the coffin and, in the flickering candlelight saw a copy of the Gospels lying on a wide shelf which covered the body. The wooden ledge hung by two rings fixed at either end, so was easily removed. When they thus exposed the body stretched out on its right side, they smelt an odour similar to that released by trampled wildflowers of the sweetest fragrance. The monks recoiled in awe as the body of Saint Cuthbert was apparently entire. The brothers gazed at each other in silent amazement and shrank back to some distance, not even Thurgot daring to gaze at the miracle. Awed whispering between nearest neighbours about what they had seen only ceased when the prior demanded repetition of the seven psalms of penitence in low voices. This activity calmed their nerves but, still reverential, they approached the coffin on their hands and knees.

Fears dispelled, they stood and Thurgot ordered tapestry and robes to be spread on the ground.

"Osbern, you place your hands under the head," he said to the sacrist, "Aldwine, you take the feet," the sub-prior gasped but obeyed, "Algar—the middle of the body." The future prior complied and the three men gently raised the body and laid it respectfully on the prepared cloths.

This operation allowed them to clear the coffin of a great number of bones within separate linen bags, the mortal remains of other bishops of Lindisfarne, all saintly men. Cuthbert had been laid on his side to make room for the bones of these and other saints. The monks reverently removed them and stored them elsewhere in the church. Now they could lay their saint on his back in the coffin; but, after much discussion, they placed the head of Saint Oswald, the martyr, between his hands. Since the hour of Matins was drawing near, they hastily closed the lid and replaced the coffin in its former location.

Prior Thurgot took charge of the chapter meeting the next morning and told the full gathering of monks of their discoveries. Amid general wonder, the only discordant note was struck by Bishop Ranulf, who refused to believe the report and declared that even a sworn statement would barely satisfy him.

Owing to the haste of the previous night, Thurgot told his assistants that they must repeat the inspection, which would now be more accessible and therefore leisurely. So, the same monks carried the body into the choir and placed it on vestments spread on the pavement. They observed that the body had been dressed in a robe of a costly kind, under which it was wrapped in a purple dalmatic, and then in linen, and all these clothes were whole and fresh without stains of corruption. By candlelight Brother Symeon strained his eyes to note all these details on parchment. He wrote a list of the objects buried with the body: scissors, an ivory comb, silver altar, paten and a small chalice.

In the face of the bishop's scepticism, Thurgot allowed himself to handle the body, raising and lowering it, to determine indisputably that it was a body in a state of incorruption,

"The sinews are still solid, my Brothers. Now, let us clothe it with the lovely pall we have brought and replace the coffin behind the altar."

The following morning, the monks were eager to announce what they had seen and then performed a solemn service of thanksgiving to proclaim their triumph and silence the incredulous.

Word spread of the discovery and people of all ranks and ages flocked to Durham from the surrounding areas. They had heard of the miracle of no decay after centuries and gloried in the fact that they were alive at the time of this revelation. The monks revelled in the reflected glory but their joy was short-lived. An abbot of a neighbouring monastery asked why the brothers had chosen darkness to visit the tomb, and why none but the monks of Durham had been present. His aspersions burst into an open accusation,

"These brothers are unworthy of belief since they would have us be satisfied with their version and no proof! I ask again that the coffin be opened before the eyes of strangers who have come to assist at the translation."

"How dare he insinuate!" the sub-prior beat his breast.

"It goes hard with me but we must have trust in our eyes and expose our beloved saint to more scrutiny," Thurgot muttered. However, he was too astute to concede access immediately.

The king, absent in Normandy, had sent his representative, the abbot of Séez, and bishop-elect of Rochester, to Durham and only when this worthy prevailed on Thurgot to accede to the reasonable demands, did he accept. He recognised that any doubt had to be removed and further examination would result in greater glory for the new cathedral and the fame of Saint Cuthbert would spread to all the world. So, he agreed that a certain number of fit persons, including the abbots, should be admitted to witness the miracle. He chose fifty and they were led into the new choir. Apart from five of the most important abbots in the land, Alexander, heir to the throne of Scotland was present. The bishop of Durham was not in attendance because he was dedicating an altar in another part of the cathedral.

The chest that enclosed the remains was placed before them and the lid removed.

Thurgot stepped before them, raised a hand and said,

"I forbid anyone to touch the body without my express permission! My brethren, ensure my order is obeyed." The Durham monks moved threateningly into position. "To our visitors, I humbly ask you to acquaint yourselves with the truth with your eyes—nothing must be removed from the coffin." The dignitaries filed past one by one lingering to ascertain what the prior had said was true. But the abbot of Séez, in virtue of his role as the king's emissary, said,

"In the name of the king, I demand to touch the body."

"You may, Father Abbot," Thurgot said without hesitation.

Richard D'Aubigny, Abbot of Séez, stepped forward officiously and seizing an arm tested the flexibility of the joint, he moved the head and the legs and finally, pulled an ear quite vigorously. He felt other parts of the body then, straightened, turned and declared,

"I have found solid sinews and bones clothed with the softness of flesh. My brethren, the body which we have before us is unquestionably dead, but it is just as sound and entire as when it was forsaken by its holy soul on its way to the heavens."

"The Lord be praised!" cried Stephen, abbot of St Mary, York.

"The Durham brothers spoke true," whispered Hugh de Lacy, abbot of St Germans, Selby to the bishop's chaplain, William de Corbeil. "It looks like I owe them my apology."

The most incredulous among them admitted he was satisfied and every doubt vanished. Prior Thurgot ordered the singing of the *Te Deum* before the actual ceremony of translation.

SEVENTEEN

DURHAM, NORTHUMBRIA 1004-11 AD

People gathered outside the new cathedral to take part in the translation ceremony and, to catch a glimpse of the saint and the crowd became so dense that the procession of Cuthbert's coffin perambulated around the edifice with great difficulty. Meanwhile, Bishop Ranulf preached a sermon on resurrection, at last proclaiming the incorruption of the saint's body. Exactly four hundred and eighteen years had passed, he explained, since Cuthbert's death. With a dramatic flourish, the bishop held up the hermit's copy of St John's Gospel and Kenrick thrilled to see the brilliant leather-working of his distant ancestor, Aella.

Prior Thurgot leant and whispered into his sub-prior's ear.

"This sermon is mostly irrelevant to this occasion and he's droning on endlessly."

"Ay, that he is, said Aldwine, "but hark! Is that not rain?"

They both looked up as the first heavy drops hit the ground. It seemed impossible because the day had been so bright with no hint of bad weather. Suddenly, the sky darkened and the rain teemed down.

"Quick!" cried the Prior, interrupting the service, "Take the saint inside!"

been achieved. He stood gazing at the shrine and wondered how he could give the place a personal imprint beyond the sheer majesty of his innovations. Nobody had created ribbed vaulting or pointed arches before him, not even in Europe, but they were not features that the ordinary man could point to and say, in hushed tones, *Look, admire the work of Master Kenrick the mason!*

He ambled slowly away pondering the problem. The choir was now empty and he passed into the vacant and three-quarters-finished nave. There, he strolled to the end, turned and stared at the stark piers and an idea came to him. He hurried to his lodgings, seized a strip of unused parchment and a piece of charcoal, sketched a pier and began to scrawl on it. Irritated, shaking his head, it would never do—something more distinctive was needed so that when a man entered the great door, the first thing to catch his eye—he turned the sheet over and tried again. This time with bold zig-zags, he had what he wanted. Ay, that was striking enough! It would be easy to incise too; sometimes, the best ideas are the simplest. He grinned at the little stray cat he'd taken in. She still didn't have a name, he'd toyed with so many, but now he'd give her an inspired one, he'd call her *Ziggy!* Strange name for a cat, but it would be his signature in the cathedral and the motif could be recurrent elsewhere!

He scooped up the ginger waif,

"It can, can't it, Ziggy?" he said, stroking the feline behind her ears and responding to the happiness seeping from her owner, she purred contentedly. He sat petting the cat and thinking about where the chevrons could be incised other than on the important piers.

"I'll try some tomorrow on somewhere not too prominent," he told his pet, which looked up at him with glowing yellow eyes, "just to get the feel of them and see the effect. But where? I know! On the jambs of the slype doorway." He lifted the protesting animal so that his face and hers were almost nose to nose and as if explaining to a friend, said, "That way, the monks will see my signature as they pass through from the transept into the corridor leading to the chapter house. Who's got a clever master, Ziggy?" The cat mewed plaintively.

"Ay, that's right, *you* have!" He set her down gently and considered the risk. What if he was wrong? What if his carving didn't create the striking impact he wanted? It might destroy the harmonious optical whole of his nave. Scrunching his eyes tight closed, he tried to imagine the visual effect.

That failed, he walked across the room to the rough wooden cross hanging from a nail.

Closing his eyes and threading his fingers so one hand clasped the other, he preferred that to steepling, he prayed.

Saint Cuthbert, I had this idea in your cathedral after standing by your shrine. Can't you tell me whether to do this or not? Send me a sign!

Kenrick recognised that he was inexpert at prayer. The irony of it! A friend of priors and monks and still, he didn't know how. Where was Cuthbert's sign? He stood for several minutes, head bowed, waiting in silence. Suddenly, there was a yowl of protest from the bored cat. When he turned, she was staring at him and her sharp teeth and claws had accounted for his parchment. He hurried over but he knew he was too late—Ziggy had shredded his chevrons! Despite the risk of scratching involved, he separated the parchment from the predator and looked at her handiwork. The crumpled image of the pier struck him at once; the rotation of the image caused casually by his pestiferous pet, produced an even more striking effect.

"That's my sign!" he cried jubilantly, "Ziggy, you little angel!" The little demon protested when he tried to scoop her up and she flew under the chair in the corner of the room and peered out at him defiantly. Taking another piece of un-shredded parchment, he set Ziggy's handiwork before him, sketched a pier again, and this time copied what he saw before him. The result was elegant and impressive and he knew that he should have laid out his chevrons like this. He glared at the cat.

"It's my ruddy idea, not yours, bloody creature!"

The undisputed master of the concept rose at first light, did without breakfast, such was his desire to test his design. By the time he had consigned his pet to the washerwoman and hurried uphill to the cathedral he was breathless and had to stop before entering, gulping in the fresh but damp morning air. A wheezing cough shook him and he bent forward hands on knees,

I'm too old to be charging around like a demented hare.

Walking into the nave, he stared at the piers and columns and visualised the effect. Ay, he would have to be subtle with such striking zig-zags. Kenrick was already hard at work at the base of a pier when his men arrived, most of them punctual as usual. There were a lot of curious questions but he told them,

"Just wait and see! And get cracking, that nave wall won't reach up to the gallery by itself!"

They knew his moods well and, grinning at each other, some set about mixing cement whilst others brought and shaped stone.

As Kenrick carved into the enclosing outer stone of the rubble-filled pier, he thought about all the places chevrons could be introduced as decoration. The list grew, including some arches, the arcade in the western bays, for instance, the bays in the gallery and the clerestory. He could not write but Thurgot was a scribe. He would convince him, ay:

I'm old and getting older. I might die tomorrow. I should leave instructions for my successor.

Determined to do this, nonetheless, he put off that conversation for a day or two, his priority being to reach the collar around the shaft before sunset. By careful measuring and accurate spacing, he had traced the twelve courses in charcoal and was confident of reaching the end by his self-imposed deadline. If he could do one pier a day, he would be busy for the next five days just on this side of the nave. Another idea came to him but he needed to see this pier from where the doorway would be, so he must press on.

Late in the afternoon, he stepped down from his ladder, brushed the dust off his hands, removed the steps for an unimpeded view of his handiwork and backed steadily to the end of the nave. Wonderful! If ever a signature made a statement this was it! Now, what about my idea? He had carved the third pier and they were alternating with columns. What if he did the same to piers five, seven, nine and eleven? By the time he reached eleven, he would be flanking the sanctuary bay. He could not simply repeat what he had done on the third pier: three sets of spirals turning in alternating directions and two shorter sets of vertical fluting—no, he needed to proceed with a more sophisticated design—he pondered and stared at his pet.

Unfortunately, his ginger tabby was no help that evening, except to soothe his troubled state by her affectionate purring. The nagging thought that he was missing something obvious tended to snatch away the solution, like a drowning man reaching for the end of a rope, desperate for salvation. This thought reminded him of how he had saved Thurgot and had him reflecting that he wouldn't be grasping for this answer if fate hadn't offered him the chance to save the monk, his best friend. So, he retired for the night with this happier thought and, perhaps, for this reason, his brain being unfathomable, he woke with a resolution in mind.

The fifth pier e would decorate with five sections of spirals and almost no vertical fluting; the seventh would have an unbroken spiral in a single direction in very low relief; the ninth and eleventh, which flank the two sanctuary bays, he would give unbroken spirals but in multiple mouldings incised in thick, deep relief, with that of the eleventh deeper than that of the ninth.

Ay, that's the solution!

Realising instinctively, although he could not have expressed it in words that his scheme would have the effect of leading the worshipper from the west end to the east with a sense of increasing intensity, culminating in the sanctuary, where the shafts would be at their richest and where they would break the pattern and be combined with decorated capitals—

Ay! ay! To create a truly dramatic effect!

Early morning suited Kenrick's creativity and he could just imagine carved capitals. He would enjoy himself carving fighting beasts, some animals playing musical instruments and if the mood took him, he'd include Ziggy the cat on one of the capitals! He'd get that promising young lad, Faruin, to carve a couple of capitals, too. The boy had shaped the wonderful head of a bearded man to accommodate a water spout.

Hurrying off to work, he stopped in the entrance as if halted by an invisible hand. His chevrons greeted him like a hearty salute and confirmed his decision. True, the first pier still had not been erected but, half closing his eyes, he could envisage the effect of the whole.

"Faruin! Come here, boy!" Such was his enthusiasm that the bellow startled the men nearest him and the youth came running, terrified that he had done something wrong to land him in the master's bad books.

A fatherly arm around his shoulder and a quiet word in his ear and the young man's face lit up with delight. Kenrick walked him to the seventh pier,

"What about starting with a nice intricate floral design on this one? Get a piece of charcoal and do a few designs for my approval."

So, life proceeded untroubled on the cathedral site and Thurgot spared Kenrick the anxieties and troubles he was enduring with Bishop Ranulf. The prelate returned from Normandy in 1005, where he had gone straight after the translation, and immediately clashed with the monks. Led by the formidable Thurgot, the monastic confraternity posed a threat to the bishop's free exercise of his authority. The long experience of ruling themselves meant that when the prelate took up residence in his palace, he encountered a community used to controlling the needs of the diocese. The prior had to resist the encroachments of Ranulf upon the possessions and privileges of the monks. The old agreement of 109, he swept aside, diverting the altar dues and the burial fees to his coffers for the completion of the cathedral nave.

Sheltered from these tensions, Kenrick was the grateful recipient of funds that enabled him to complete the nave walls up to the vaulting. Although he was titular abbot, Flambard was not a monk and, so, could not take part in monastic routine. Unlike Thurgot, he had not gazed upon the face of Cuthbert. The result was that he had to resist the powerful growing cult of the saint, which dominated the monks' lives. The bishop was an intelligent man and could not sustain such an untenable position for long. Screened from this situation, Kenrick may have been, but when it came to a head, he was affected very sorely.

EIGHTEEN

DURHAM, NORTHUMBRIA 1105 AD

P<small>RIOR</small> T<small>HURGOT</small> <small>GAZED</small> <small>UNSEEINGLY</small> <small>AS</small> <small>THE</small> <small>MESSENGER</small> departed his residence since his mind was transporting him back to Melrose many years before. She had been known to him then as Edith but now was Queen of England and went by the name of Matilda. Many of her subjects labelled her *Mathilda bona regina* as she was a woman of exceptional holiness, fit to rival her mother in piety. Queen Matilda was renowned for her generosity towards the Church, founding and supporting cloisters and hospitals for lepers. At Lent, she attended services barefoot and people spoke fondly of how she washed the feet and kissed the hands of the sick.

She had contacted him after many years, imploring him to write a biography of her mother, Margaret of Scotland. Of course, he had accepted the task largely due to the strong relationship he had built up with the saintly woman in the years 1086-7 when the bishop of Durham was away and in 1088-91 when the prelate was living in exile in Normandy. The education of the royal children, including Edith, fell to him and he had freely given advice in connection with Margaret's new monastery in Dunfermline. In 1092, he had been instrumental in giving permanence to the relationship between the

Scottish throne and the Durham community. The monks of Saint Cuthbert agreed with Malcolm and Margaret to feed one poor man each day, and two on Maundy Thursday, and to say a collect for them at the Litany. So, given all that, he could not refuse and the messenger returned with his assent to York, where the queen was staying.

Besides, Thurgot believed that Matilda's request had befallen the right person; she could hardly have chosen a more sympathetic — and God forgive his presumption, more erudite—biographer. Thinking that there was no time like the present, he sauntered to the scriptorium lost in his memories. Selecting the best vellum, he took a quill, dipped it in ink and settled to begin his task. Fluently writing two paragraphs of formal introduction, he came to the point:

I congratulate you, in that, being appointed queen of the Angles by the king of the angels, you desire not only to hear the life of the queen your mother, who ever aspired to the realm of angels but also to have it constantly before you in writing: so that, although you knew but little your mother's face, you may have more fully the knowledge of her virtues.

He laid down the pen and, sitting back, sighed heavily. Twelve years had passed since the queen's soul had flown to paradise and he missed her sorely, for she had been as beautiful within as without. Would the Lord guide his hand so that he might worthily convey the virtues of so great a woman? Reflecting on the name, Margaret, he picked up the quill, charged it with ink and wrote about how the meaning of the name in Hebrew was *pearl*:

The pearl has been taken to the Lord. The pearl, I repeat, has been taken from the dungheap of this world; and glows now, set in the diadem of the eternal king. No one will doubt this, when he has heard, a little further on, of her life and her life's end.

With his sleeve, he wiped away the tear forming in his eye at the memory of his regal friend. It would never do to weep onto his ink lest it blot and he had to start over again. What had she seen in him?

He remembered that she saw him as a saintly man, but he told her continually that there was nothing saintly in him.

The ease with which he embraced distraction irked him; he glanced at his fellow scribes, each immersed in the work in front of him and not allowing his gaze to wander as idly as his. Clicking his tongue, he set about writing of the queen's noble ancestry, for that would not stir his emotions in the same way. With pleasure, he described her grandfather, King Edmund, whose valour had earned him the name *Ferreum-latus*—the Ironside— before referring to that king's brother, the gentle and wise King Edward, the Confessor, who, he set down, protected the kingdom rather with peace than with arms. Thurgot wrote, eyes fixed on his parchment until his wrist ached, praising Margaret's forebears thanks to his profound knowledge of their reigns— for had he not written his *Historia Regum Anglorum*, the History of the Kings of England? — before ending:

...King Edmund, whose son's daughter, Margaret, with the glory of her merits greatly adorns the glorious line of her ancestors.

Unlike the other monks in the scriptorium, the prior had different demands on his time, so he scattered powder on the wet ink, shook it off and placed his parchment aside for safekeeping because the next day he would set down how she began her earliest youth.

As prior, there were other pressing matters to deal with, he had to battle with the avid bishop of Durham, his by now constant adversary. Ranulf Flambard would stop at nothing to finance the cathedral building, which in itself, Thurgot approved of, for had he not been himself responsible for many years for funding Kenrick's work? But he, the prior, had never stooped, like Ranulf, to misappropriation. Inevitably, the clash would be heated and unpleasant since the peculation involved cemetery fees rightly destined to the monastic community. When confronted with his embezzlement, the bishop fell back on justifying his actions for the greater glory of God.

"It's hardly a case of my lavishing money on personal extravagancies." He would say although Thurgot knew that the prelate made sure his wine cellar and his pantry were well stocked.

Several of the monks seized the coffin and hastily conveyed it into the new cathedral. Immediately, the storm ceased.

The sub-prior whispered to Thurgot,

"Extraordinary What do you make of that?"

More level-headed than many of his brethren, Thurgot shrugged and said,

"What should I make of it? A brief but heavy shower."

There could be no disputing that, but many of the brothers were already murmuring that the storm was Cuthbert's displeasure at being turned into a long-winded spectacle. Thurgot thought it nonsense but he could not explain how his habit was not wet after he had been drenched outside.

At last, the body of the saint was placed in its prepared resting place in the apse. It was a structure of stone, built behind the high altar and raised higher to be reached by steps to the platform, on which Kenrick had erected nine three-foot-high columns supporting a finely decorated marble slab bearing the coffin. The monks, too, had played their part, enveloping the sacred body in new splendid vestments so that everything was ready for the performance of a solemn mass.

But first, Prior Thurgot decided to make a late adjustment to the coffin and climbed onto the marble slab. He invited Abbot Richard of St Albans to help him, but the abbot had a paralysed left hand. Nonetheless, he joined the prior to aid him and when he touched the coffin with the injured hand, suddenly, all feeling and movement returned — the monks present testified to yet another miracle.

During the mass, from the body of the church, voices, echoing from the splendid choir vaults, were raised in praise before everyone returned home with joy, glorifying and praising God and Saint Cuthbert for what they had seen and heard.

Finally, Thurgot could relax since everything had proceeded favourably for himself and the cathedral. So too, could Kenrick, the purpose of his life was complete, so he could die content. His masterpiece was still unfinished but its true magnificence and scope had

After the impassioned and at times vehement exchange, the prior succeeded in reclaiming the missing fees even if he suspected that the accounting had been falsified by several crucial omissions. The partial triumph, realistically, was the best he could achieve. Knowing how much his defence of the monastic community irritated the bishop, he decided that on this occasion it was wiser not to press the point.

The next morning, he hurried from Prime to take up his quill to describe the dedication of the young princess to her religious studies. He ended the section with heartfelt praise:

Nothing was firmer than her faith, more constant than her countenance, more enduring than her patience, more important than her advice, juster than her opinion, pleasanter than her conversation.

The prior laid down the pen and reread his words. He reflected, he certainly was eulogising but his text was for posterity and should also serve as an example to the reader, the daughter of the flawless queen of Scotland. On the morrow, he would write about Margaret's marriage and her behaviour towards the Church.

At the moment, he would have to be about his duties as prior. Unfortunately, unlike the scribes, he could not sit for hours to expedite this work. But bless them, he had them copying books for the library or, in the case of the promising Brother Brunulf, writing an account of the translation of Saint Cuthbert and the subsequent miracles at his shrine. The scribe was numbering the miracles and at present was at miracle number 12. During miracle 10 Thurgot was prior and whilst Brunulf seldom mentioned him by name, in 10 he called him *praepositus monasterii*—the prior of the monastery— and in 11 *praepositus memortus*—the renowned prior—this pleased Thurgot, who regularly checked the scribe's work although he sought no fame for himself. It did, however, give him some satisfaction that the monk portrayed him as a prior full of active concern for everyone he encountered.

Before returning to his commitments, Thurgot, as was often his wont, ambled over to Brunulf's desk and asked solicitously what he was writing.

"How goes it, Brother, what is your theme today?"

"You will remember Prior because you took part in the miracle of the silken band." The young monk, who somewhat hero-worshipped the prior, turned his parchment so that the monk could read it in comfort without craning his neck.

The miracle occurred during the long sermon at the translation when Bishop Ranulf showed the people Cuthbert's copy of St John's Gospel taken from the coffin. The book was enclosed in a leather satchel with a much-frayed silken band, by which, in his life, it was hung around the saint's neck. One of Flambard's officials removed a thread and hid it in his shoe, but the following night, he suffered severe pain and a swollen leg.

Thurgot nodded his head and muttered to himself,

"That was when the rascal came to me, limping and using a staff for support." He laughed and turning to the young scribe, whose account had been interrupted at that point by the prior's arrival, he said,

"You write it true. If my memory serves, the scoundrel brought the silken thread and offered it to me." The prior grunted, "I insisted that it must be returned personally to the saint. I remember as if it were yesterday how his eyes filled with fear and he begged that some of the brothers accompanied him. They obliged and the fellow prayed to Cuthbert for forgiveness at the shrine, at which, as you know, Brother Brunulf, he was restored to perfect health. Now, I must leave you. Good work! Finish it well and may the saint bless your eyes!"

The prior strolled along the arcaded cloister towards his cell and glanced casually at the well. Unhooking the swinging bucket, Brother Eolf, one of the oldest monks in the community, took the weight and stepped over to the cistern to empty the pail. Thurgot heard his groan, saw his face contort and watched the bucket fall to the grass, whilst the elderly monk clutched his chest, tottered and sank to the ground. The prior rushed over to the brother but with anguish, saw that there was nothing to be done. Eolf's heart had failed, likely under the strain of hauling the heavy pail.

Silently, Thurgot cursed the bishop of Durham. He had been petitioning him for months for the funds to lay a lead piping conduit from freshwater springs identified on the west side of the Wear. His pleas, falling on deaf ears, had met a stone wall of indifference. The laver had already been built in the corner of the cloister and ready to receive running water. Bishop Ranulf was determined that all construction money would be spent only on the cathedral, so the prelate's attitude, as the gathering brethren were quick to point out, was directly responsible for the demise of the white-haired Eolf.

They pressed Thurgot to take the matter up with the bishop once more and so he would, but first, he needed to pray that the irremovable prelate would have a change of heart.

In the audience, when it became clear that no such reorientation would occur, Thurgot's patience snapped.

"Don't you realise that your attitude has cost our dear brother his life?"

"Dare you address your bishop in this way, Prior? And shabbily seek to transfer your grave fault to another?"

"*My* fault?" Thurgot could scarcely believe his ears, his face puce with rage, he roared,

"How can it be *my* fault?"

"Examine your conscience, Prior Thurgot—if you had devised a roster involving only the younger monks to draw water, the old man would be alive today. I suggest you seek your confessor and fulfil penance for your negligence."

Thurgot glared at the bishop, spun on his heel without waiting to be dismissed and marched back to the monastery.

The man is a sanctimonious sinner unworthy to carry the crozier!

Once more, he had failed to obtain the funding for the conduit, but he swore he would not give up. Deciding to let the emotional passing of Eolf's death die down because he did not want to lead a revolt, he would try again in the months ahead.

After Eolf's burial the next day, he returned to the scriptorium and adjusted his parchment to continue his *Life of Saint Margaret*.

He remembered that her first thought as the new queen was to erect a noble church in the place of her marriage, dedicated to the Holy Trinity. Its purpose was the redemption of the king's soul and her own, also, so that her children would prosper in this life and the one to come. She ornamented the church richly, with vessels of solid gold for the ministry of the altar. Thurgot had seen this with his own eyes and wrote about:

...a cross of incomparable value, she placed there, bearing the Saviour's image; she had it all overlaid with purest gold and silver, with jewels set here and there between; even today it proves clearly to beholders the devoutness of her faith.

Thurgot wrote throughout the morning, wilfully setting aside other business as he immersed himself in a description of Margaret's upbringing of her children and then of her zealous reading habits, which she ensured others followed for their salvation. Remembering his other obligations, the prior ceased his writing, promising himself to proceed the next day with the queen's conferral of honour and glory on the kingdom of the Scots.

He decided to go to the cathedral, but more particularly to Cuthbert's shrine, where he wished to pray for forgiveness for the angry and wicked thoughts he had harboured towards the bishop since the death of Eolf.

Sometimes, at our most negative towards someone, divine intervention, couched most subtly, helps us to modify our opinion. This happened to the prior as he encountered his friend, the master mason in one of the aisles.

"Good morning, Kenrick, how is your work proceeding?"

"Mornin', Thurgot!" the mason bestowed his usual cheery beam on greeting him, "well, thank you. Come and see what you think of this." He led his friend to the aisle walls of the presbytery and proudly displayed the interlaced arcading forming a dado that came up to the height of Thurgot's chest. A mason was working on the end section as he looked on.

"So, what do you think?"

"I think it's exquisite, but where do you get your wonderful ideas?"

"I'll be honest with you. This ain't my idea, Thurgot. It's an Islamic design."

The prior laughed uneasily, out of surprise,

"But if you've never been to Iberia or the Arabian lands!"

"Nay, it's true, but our bishop has, and he noted and sketched it for me. He even suggested I place it here as a dado. Well, I could see at once that he was right—inspired, I'd say!"

Grudgingly, Thurgot had to give Flambard his due. It was lovely and blended perfectly with the rest of the cathedral decoration.

"I must go and pray at the shrine."

This he did, making sure to beg forgiveness for his dislike of the bishop and admitting his admiration for the prelate's contribution to the cathedral. However, he also prayed for guidance in the matter of the water conduit.

Over the next few days, he made great progress with his *Vita S. Margaritae Reginae*. First, he wrote how he corrected the things her people did contrary to the faith and the custom of the holy Church and induced them to observe the rules. Later, although he did not know as he sat there carefully forming his letters, he would have a first-hand experience of these thorny problems. For the moment, his hand sped inspired by the queen's compunction to prayer and fasting and works of mercy. He listed many examples of her compassion for the poor. That done, with Queen Matilda in mind, he wrote about how her mother acted before the Lord's Nativity, and in Lent.

After several days of writing, Prior Thurgot groaned and stared blankly at his densely-covered parchment. True, he had written much about the queen's *rising from virtue to virtue*, but now he was blocked. He searched his mind for what else he could add to this *Life*. He felt it was too short, too soon to write about her death.

Whenever he was in serious difficulty, with anything, not only writing, he resorted to prayer and so, once again he visited Cuthbert's shrine. As usual, inspiration came. He needed a new approach: not what Queen Margaret displayed for God, but the exact opposite. Almost tripping over a workman's carelessly abandoned shovel, he hurried out of the cathedral back to the scriptorium where his quill seemed to take over his wrist, flying across the vellum:

Let us more worthily hold her in awe, because through her devotion to justice, piety, mercy and love, we contemplate in her, rather than miracles, the deeds of the ancient fathers.

Thurgot humbly wrote this about Margaret without it ever occurring to him that he might have applied the same words to himself and perhaps, for this reason, the Queen of Scotland saw in him what he failed to see.

NINETEEN

DURHAM, NORTHUMBRIA, 1105 AD

PRIOR THURGOT RETURNED TO HIS DESK AT THE SCRIPTORIUM intending to set down the facts surrounding Queen Margaret's death. Even as he took his seat, he realised that in his mind he could not separate this event from the death of her husband, Malcolm. Yet, he did not wish to write about *that* unworthy man in his *Life of Queen Margaret*. Instead, he ignored his quill and sat thinking about the savage king that the great woman had to a great extent civilised. He ran through his knowledge of the reign until he arrived at the year leading up to the queen's demise.

The prior recalled that in 1092, the shaky peace between England and the Scots began to break down. The Scots controlled much of Cumbria, but William Rufus's new castle at Carlisle and his settlement of English peasants in the surrounding area was only one of causes of the dispute. Thurgot knew for sure, because he was in charge of the diocese at the time, that the contested ownership of estates granted to Malcolm by William I in 1072, for his maintenance when visiting England, was another reason for strife. Malcolm sent messengers to discuss the question and William Rufus agreed to a meeting. Malcolm travelled south to Gloucester, stopping at Wilton

Abbey to visit his daughter, Edith and sister-in-law, Cristina. The king of the Scots arrived there on 24 August 1093 to find that William Rufus refused to negotiate, insisting that the dispute be judged by the English barons. This Malcolm refused to accept unless their Scottish peers sat in judgement, too. This proposal was rejected, so he returned immediately to Scotland.

The prior had little sympathy for Malcolm and his fate because he could remember as if it were yesteryear how he gathered an army, and came harrowing into England...Thurgot said out loud, "with more hostility than behoved him!" causing the monk at the next desk to raise his head and dart him a surprised glance. But it was true, even by the cruel standards of the prior's time, the laying waste of Northumbria by the ravaging Scots was seen as harsh.

Malcolm rode into battle with Edward, his eldest son by Margaret and heir-designate, and by Edgar, the queen's brother. While marching north again, Malcolm was ambushed by Robert de Mowbray, Earl of Northumbria, whose lands he had devastated, near Alnwick on 13 November 1093. There he was killed by Arkil Morel, steward of Bamburgh Castle. Thurgot remembered everyone rejoicing and treating the steward as a hero. Edward was mortally wounded in the same Battle of Alnwick.

Thurgot sighed heavily. He could not possibly have written this in his *Life,* but he was obliged to mention the terrible effect the tragedy had on Queen Margaret, for she died of sorrow for the loss of her beloved husband within nine days.

Thurgot expertly dipped his quill in the inkwell and remembering a conversation that he had shared with the queen before her death, wrote,

"Farewell" she said, "I shall not continue much longer in this life; and thou wilt live a long time after me." He smiled grimly, she was right, the first signs of grey hair had appeared at his temples. "There are two things I request of thee: one, that thou remember my soul in thy masses and prayers all thy life; the other, that thou take charge of my sons and daughters, and afford them love; and especially teach them, and never cease to teach them, to fear and love God." Having set that down, Thurgot re-read it and reflected,

I suppose I have kept my promise and fulfilled her wishes to the best of my ability. After that conversation, I never saw her again.

Not long after that exchange, the queen suffered a debilitating disease and Thurgot decided to relate her death as he had heard it from her priest. He started to write, word for word, what the priest had told him, straining his memory so that he reproduced the exact speech:

*For half a year and somewhat more, she was never able to sit on horseback; and seldom to rise from her bed. On the fourth day before her death, while the king was upon an expedition, and she could not have known from the swiftness of any messenger what was happening to him on that day, at so great a distance away over the land, she became suddenly sadder, and said this to us who sat beside her: 'Per-*haps today so great an evil has happened to the kingdom of the Scots, as has not happened for many ages past.'

When we heard this, we received her words with little attention at the time; but after some days a messenger arrived, and we learned that the king had been killed on the same day upon which the queen had thus spoken. As if foreseeing the future, she had strongly opposed his going with any army; but it happened, I know not for what reason, that on this occasion he did not obey her warnings.

*When the fourth day after the slaying of the king arrived, her infirmity being somewhat lightened, she entered the oratory, to hear mass; and there she took care to prepare for her death, which was already imminent, with the sacred **viaticum** of the body and blood of the Lord. After having been revived by the salutary gust of these, she was presently troubled with a return of her former pains; and was prostrated in bed: and, as the malady increased, she was driven violently on towards her death.*

The Prior, overcome with emotion, and amazed at the queen's prescience, laid down his pen and studied a couple of blackbirds bobbing around the cloister, allowing them to distract him from his sorrowful memories. As he gazed at the songbirds, he considered that his memory had been reliable and now, he recalled an important detail that felt obliged to set down. Quickly taking up his quill, he described the arrival of her son, returning from the war to announce to his mother that his father and brother had been slain; and *he found that his mother was on the brink of death. On all sides grief, on all sides pain, had entangled him. While the queen, lying as in agony, was thought by those present to be dead, she suddenly rallied her strength and addressed her son. She questioned him about his father and brother; but he would not tell her the truth, lest hearing of their death she too should instantly die: so he answered that they were well. But she sighed deeply, and said, 'I know, my son, I know. I adjure thee by this holy cross, by the nearness of our relationship, to speak out what thou knowest to be true.' He was compelled to disclose the matter as it had occurred.*

Thurgot took a new sheet of vellum and steeled himself for the hardest part of the task Queen Matilda had set him—to relate the actual moment of her mother's passing. It had to be done, so he wrote,

At the same time she had lost her husband, she had lost a son, disease had tortured her to death: but in all this she sinned not with her lips; she spoke no foolish word against God. Instead, she raised her eyes and her hands to heaven, and broke into praise and thanksgiving, saying: 'I render praises and thanks to thee, almighty God, who hast willed that I should endure such anguish at my death; and to cleanse me, as I hope, by enduring it, from some stains of sin.'

Thurgot bit his lower lip, failing to recall the exact words referred to him about her last prayer but he remembered the salient point:

While she was saying 'deliver me', her soul was released from the chains of the body, and departed to Christ, whom she had always loved...

The prior continued to write and praise the saintly queen for the calmness and tranquillity of her death and to eulogise her as a shining example to follow.

Finally, with a sense of having achieved his purpose to his satisfaction, he described the enshrouding and burial of the body in the church she had commanded built, the Holy Trinity, opposite the altar and the holy cross. Thurgot concluded his *Life* with these words:

And thus her body now rests in the place where she used to afflict it with vigils and prayers, with shedding tears and bowing of knees.

Prior Thurgot shed tears, too, at the memory of his royal friend's premature end, he sighed,

Some people should never die: their loss is too unbearable.

He thought, as he carefully gathered the pages, fruit of many days' labour, rolled them tidily and bound them with a silk ribbon. Queen Matilda would decide whether they were worthy, as he hoped, to be stitched and bound into a book.

To distract his sorrowful thoughts, he strolled over to his favourite young scribe, Brother Brunulf, to see what he was writing.

"How goes it, Brother?"

"Ah, Prior, I am describing another miracle of our saint that occurred lately. You will most certainly have it in mind. I'm calling it miracle 16. It happened in 1094."

"Ay, a year after Queen Margaret's departure," Thurgot murmured, more to himself as his account was fresh in his mind. "Remind me of it, Brother."

"They were building the cathedral in the early stages and wood was needed for the work. So, men took eight bullocks to fetch a huge log up—"

"I remember that occasion and the miraculous occurrence."

The monk smiled but felt inclined to relate the happening, none-theless.

"Ay, fetching it uphill towards Durham, when a child, a boy, skip-ping along gaily beside the chained log, fell and his leg ended under the heavy trunk. Everyone feared his limb would be crushed and sixteen men were needed to lift the log and release the child, who skipped along again as though nothing had happened. The people who witnessed the event all swore that it must certainly have been a prodigy of Saint Cuthbert; otherwise, the child by rights ought never to have walked again."

"The Lord and Saint Cuthbert be praised!" cried Thurgot.

"Amen!"

He walked away from the cloister as if, by finishing his *Vita S. Margaritae Reginae,* the weight of that log had been removed from his shoulders. As he strolled away, he prayed that he might emulate the saintly queen's patience in his dealings with Bishop Ranulf Flambard, but he feared that he was nowhere near her sanctity and that his forebearance would be sorely tested by the bishop's unsavoury character.

TWENTY

DURHAM, NORTHUMBRIA 1105 AD

The chill in the air presaged the onset of bad weather and Kenrick studied the sky before calling to his trusted head carpenter, Hailwin.

"You'd best start dismantling the stone-dressing sheds hard up against the transept walls and reconstruct them here by the northern wall as far as we've reached."

"Are you getting ready for rainy weather, Master Kenrick."

"That's what my nose tells me is coming."

Hailwin laughed,

"I ain't ever known that great snout to be wrong!"

The master mason grinned at his long-time assistant,

"It's as well to be ready because if it does set in, there's plenty can be done under cover. The nearer the sheds to our work, the better. Have you seen, Master Geldulf?"

"He was here earlier chafing at one of his carters for not keeping his waggon as he ought. If there's a worse-tempered—"

"Let it be! He's a good man and keeps his carters in order, he doesn't take any slacking. I can't complain. I need to talk to him, so if you see him, send him my way."

"Ay, I will. Now for them sheds..."

Kenrick watched with satisfaction as he hurried away. They had mutual respect and an easy working relationship. He had full control over the design of templates and Hailwin prepared them to his requirements unquestioningly. Over the last year, he had made him prepare the mouldings for the column bases, voussoirs of arches and the tracery for arcades and windows. This was done with never a cross word between them. All of the masters respected him but only the good-natured Hailwin did not discuss his decisions.

A heavy sigh escaped him. No one had ever commented on his age, except the disgraced Askold, who rotted in the castle dungeon until the Devil had snatched him from this world. But Kenrick could not fool himself, the years of responsibility had taken their toll. His position demanded the coordination of a large labour force of masons, stone cutters, carters, setters, quarrymen, carpenters, smiths, plumbers, glaziers and unskilled labourers. Just thinking about the various artisans he had to chivvy made him weary, but he strode over to the on-site forge and bellowed at the smith,

"Master Crosmund, will you inspect the building tools and see what needs a new shaft, sharpening or replacing? There's a good fellow."

Receiving the usual friendly grin and nod cheered him out of the threatened gloomy mood.

What else did he have to see to? Ah, yes, the carter! They urgently needed to increase the loads from the quarry before the tracks became muddy and made haulage impossible. He wanted to finish the north transept to the triforium before Christmas. He sighed again, knowing very well that he would not live to see the vaulting of that transept. Surely, it was only a few years away but he was weary and, in any case, the new master mason would be able to copy his choir vaulting. Smugness was not one of his characteristics but he allowed himself a self-satisfied smile at the thought of the choir vaulting. To solve that one had been tricky, he had resorted to diagonal ribs made semi-circular so that the transverse arches were stilted to achieve the same height. The north transept vaulting should not present problems of that nature, so whoever assumed his position, his successor, would not face similar difficulties.

No, it was nothing of the sort that bothered him. Now, in his sixty-fifth year, he had almost completed *his* cathedral, but it was the little signatory touches that he wanted and might not be alive to admire. At all costs, he must transmit his desires to Prior Thurgot. The serious monk would ensure that his wishes were respected.

With this in mind, he went to the monastery and found his friend.

"Brother Thurgot," he dispensed with the formal title based on familiarity, "I must talk to you, it's important."

Thurgot knew the mason so well that he sensed a weighty matter was in the offing.

"What's bothering you, my friend?"

"It's like this..." the hesitation made the prior frown, noting that the master was troubled.

"Do you need a strong drink to loosen your tongue?"

"Nay, I know what I want to say, it's just that I don't have your way with words."

"Well, don't dress them up. Come on, out with it!"

"Ay, well, it's like this, I may not have long for this world—"

Shocked, Thurgot, an otherwise patient listener, blurted,

"Why? Are you unwell?"

The grey head shook and a note of annoyance crept into the deep voice,

"I told you I'm no good with words but if you keep on butting in... nay, I'm not ill. Not *today*. But I'm growing old and weary. I fear I'll not see my cathedral finished."

Thurgot did not want to interrupt again, but in the face of the grim expression, said,

"It's just the weather getting you down, the change of season. It's in all our bones: the normal, aches and pains. You're as strong as an ox. I wish I had half your strength."

"That's as may be, Prior, but I want you to promise me something."

Shrewd as ever, Thurgot had not missed the use of his title, which meant the request was to be taken seriously.

He laid a hand on the muscular, knotted forearm,

"Anything in my power I will do, old friend."

"Thurgot, it means so much to me. It's not vanity, but I've put my soul into yon cathedral and I want it finished by my hand, not by that of another man."

The prior was unsure of his impression, but the gleam in the master's eye, was that a tear?

"What must I do?"

"Write down my ideas for completion, lest I never get the work done myself."

"Then we must away to the scriptorium. You have never been there, Kenrick."

The prior knew very well that his friend could neither read nor write. What use to him was a scriptorium? But what did it matter? Even if the monastery had possessed a copy of Euclid's *Elements of Geometry*, the master mason would not have been able to profit by it. He didn't need to. The knowledge Kenrick had accumulated was all there in that grey-haired head. The theoretical basis of any design was up there and he could work squares, circles and triangles to produce the wonderful lines and points of the structure. The cathedral five minutes away, was proof of that. The talent of his friend was that he used proportions not only to ensure the stability of the edifice but also to create its magnificence. So, he was, thought Thurgot, quite right and entitled to safeguard the correct completion of his conception in the case of his incapacity or death. But how would the master mason take the news he'd been holding back even from his sub-prior? He would do Kenrick's bidding, then break the tidings gently to him.

They had arrived at the cloister. Only the monks had the key to the slype doorway, so Kenrick's return to the cathedral would be by the quick route. The scriptorium was situated in the cloister simply because funds had dried up and the natural light was sufficient to work by, although unfortunately, not with the illumination of this grey sky.

"What is it that I must write, old friend?"

Kenrick frowned. Where to start?

"First, write down that there must be no wooden roof. The south transept roof is temporary. It must be vaulted in stone and the northern transept too. He can copy the choir vaulting there."

"Easy, easy! I can't write as fast as you can talk...copy... the choir... vaulting," he repeated slowly, "What else?"

"The nave main arcades..." ...he elaborated and the prior's quill scribbled down the instructions, "Then there's a problem with the south transept... if I had to do it, it'd be done like this, write ...ready?... The central clerestory pier will have to be cut to allow the ribs...set this down... it's important, the structure will have to be supported from small tunnel vaults over the passageway."

Since the prior had looked up perplexed, Kenrick explained carefully what this meant and how it was to be done and his friend added three more lines of explanation.

"Is that everything?"

The countenance of the master mason suddenly resembled that of one of his sculpted lions, ay, the one with the thorn in its paw,

"Everything? Nay! Yon's a cathedral, not a bl—oops, sorry!" He bit off his oath and looked sheepishly at the scribes his roar had disturbed, "A gable must be built at the west end so that the western towers can be erected. Write that the bishop's ideas for those are fine and should be respected."

Thurgot gave him a sour look,

"Hold, did you say the bishop's ideas?"

"Ay, Bishop Ranulf has travelled in Normandy and seen the latest buildings. The bishop's a smart fellow. He knows what he wants and I agree. Of course, the decorations are my preserve. Talking about which," here Kenrick grasped Thurgot's shoulder and squeezed, the prior winced,

"Ay, I'm listening; no need to cripple me!"

The pressure relented, Kenrick chortled,

"This may seem like a foolish whim, but it's of great importance to me...I want the chevron pattern repeated in the mouldings of the triforium arches, the clerestory windows and the vaulting ribs, too. Don't write this, friend, I want to confess that these zig-zags are like my signature but to be harmonious as a whole, these must be done. You will see to it, won't you?"

The master mason's plaintive voice conveyed his anxiety,

Thurgot looked up sheepishly. Soon, he would have to break his news and his old friend's heart. For the moment he mumbled something deliberately incoherent and then said clearly,

"Aught else?"

"Nay, that'll be all for now. Mind, there'll be much more added to my cathedral before all you monks, bishops, and bl—oops," he bit off another oath, "better I shut my trap! I ought to be getting back. I want to put up the first pier in the nave before nightfall, the base is already in place, so it can be done with a willing team of masons."

"Hold, for I have something to tell you, old friend," the prior's tone was solemn and he was indicating that it must be said elsewhere. But first, he threw white powder over his ink and then shook it away before conducting Kenrick into the corridor leading from the cloister to the slype door.

"Kenrick, all is not well..." he let his grim tone serve to gain the master's complete attention, the man seemed distracted, but now he was listening, "it may be that you have entrusted this parchment to the wrong man."

"How so?"

"Don't mention this to anyone else, for nothing is yet certain. I may have to leave Durham."

The effect on his old friend was as he had feared, a thunderbolt to the heart.

The reply came choked,

"But why, Thurgot? You can't leave!"

"If the king commands, I must obey."

"But why would King Henry order that?"

"Because of your *smart fellow.*"

Kenrick looked baffled then understood in a flash,

"Bishop Ranulf?"

"Ay, the very same."

"But why?"

"Because I'm a thorn in his side. We don't see eye to eye over many things—"

"But he's always seen I lack for nothing..."

"You are right, old friend, but to pay for your nave, he keeps the monks in difficulty. Just one example, you saw the scriptorium today, does it seem right to you that we have to make do in the cloister when every other monastery in the land has a separate purpose-built scriptorium?"

"So, you won't help me for that reason?" the mason growled.

Thurgot looked anguished.

"I didn't say I won't help you. Surely you know me better than that? Nay, if I remain here, I'll see to it but if they send me away—"

"They can't do that!"

"Of course, they *can.* The bishop can't wait to get rid of me and you should know that I have become close to the Queen of the Scots. Margaret would have me in her land and the bishop of Durham has seized on this to persuade King Henry. Lucky for me, the king is, as yet, not convinced. He has not always held our prelate in the highest regard. But don't worry, Kenrick if I leave, I will pass your instructions to my sub-prior, Aldwine. You know him, he's a good man and one who adores your work."

But Kenrick *did* worry as he bustled through the slype door into the cathedral. Not so much because he didn't trust Aldwine because he did, but he fretted about his life without his best friend. He had chosen to eschew women. The thought of life in Durham without Thurgot was unbearable. He would be alone, respected, ay, with plenty of friendly faces but no other real comrade he could confide in. The only companion he had was Ziggy, his ginger tabby, and she was fiercely independent at times.

In an attempt to throw off his melancholy mood, he threw himself into the erection of the first pier. His plan to be realised in the next few days was to incise this pier with deep chevrons, as deep as the eleventh and final one. In this way, the visual impact on entering the great western doorway, once it was built—and damn it! In the scriptorium, he'd forgotten to stipulate chevrons around the doorway arch. He'd tell the prior when next their paths crossed. All these pier chevrons he'd order painted very soon, in alternating bands of red and black, and then they'd see the spectacle he'd intended with his brilliant idea.

Ach, Kenrick, pride is a sin! I'm becoming vainglorious in my old age.

Back home, inconsolable, Kenrick tried to work through the implications of what Prior Thurgot had told him. A word from the king and the prior would be sent to Scotland. He knew next to nothing about the affairs of the monastery, but wasn't the prior indispensable? It had been his friend responsible for almost all the progress made on the cathedral up to now. True, there had been a brief bleak period when funds had been short, but even then, the prior had made sacrifices and enabled him to pay his creditors. Recently, he had to admit, the bishop had ensured ample coin for progress on the nave and, as a result, Kenrick was going ahead at a great pace. Might he not speak to the bishop in Thurgot's favour? What a stupid idea! Not only was he lacking eloquence, to say the least, but also he would be well and truly overstepping the mark. A craftsman was lucky if he could greet the bishop politely, let alone interfere in his decisions. That poor scheme put to rest, Kenrick contemplated a future without his friend. Could he go with him? What! And abandon his life's work at this crucial juncture? Unthinkable!

But were Thurgot to depart, would he, the Master of Durham Cathedral, the Master of the Chevron, have the will to go on living?

That was the question. He stared at the floor and pondered. Despite his years of frequenting monks, he wasn't what he would call a religious man. But even he knew that taking one's life was a dreadful sin. In any case, he was not given to such weakness, especially with his cathedral to keep him busy. Weary, ay: suicidal, a ringing *nay*!

On his pallet that night, he tossed and turned, bringing disgruntled protests from his cat, which had taken to creeping up and snuggling next to him at night. His dreams, or rather, nightmares involved collapsing vaults and the hideous tormenting face of Askold, mocking him in front of bishops and kings gathered to inspect the disaster. More than once, he woke to experience the relief that he was only dreaming, but the last nightmare was the worse.

He had built a tall spire and was inspecting the inside of the construction, but when he wished to return to the ground, his ladder had been removed. He tried calling at the top of his voice but nobody came. When he looked down from his precarious support beam, the only person below was Prior Thurgot but when he called for help the prior simply grinned, waved and walked away. How could his best friend behave in that way? He yelled down after him but the monk turned, looked up, grinned again and put his forefinger to his lips in a hushing gesture. Then he waved again and was gone.

Kenrick woke up with a shout and his furry friend flying off the rumpled covers to safety. Another bad dream! But even his untutored mind understood the significance of this one. Quite simply, he would have to come to terms with Thurgot's departure *if* it happened. Now, he had better get some sleep because on the morrow there were deep chevrons to carve.

TWENTY-ONE

DURHAM, NORTHUMBRIA, 1007 AD

AFTER DAYS OF PREVARICATION, MUCH AS HE WANTED TO AVOID Bishop Ranulf, the moment had come for Prior Thurgot to seek an audience. The lack of fresh flowing water in the monastery had reached a point where the monks were growing exasperated. Money was sorely needed for work on a conduit, for the brothers had identi- fied freshwater springs. After the translation of Saint Cuthbert's remains in 1104, offerings had increased so the brethren felt now there were no financial restraints to stop funding for their water prob- lem. It fell to the prior to take up the matter with the bishop.

"Your Grace, after the death of poor Brother Eolf, the brethren are restless and there are murmurings of neglect. Fresh water is a primary need and they see daily contributions to the cathedral thanks to the blessed presence of our saint."

The prelate looked at the monk with barely disguised distaste: how he longed to be rid of the interfering obstacle to his plans and he had contrived to achieve just that for a twelvemonth.

"*Your* saint?" Prior, "Mind your tongue! Saint Cuthbert belongs to the whole diocese and his resting place is the cathedral, which is *my* preserve, not that of the brothers."

"May I remind Your Grace that Saint Cuthbert was a simple monk and a hermit—one of us— and he eschewed the world of material splendour."

"Times change, Prior. You will have no difficulty in understanding what our saint represents to the people of this northern land. The construction of the cathedral is in part also due to your commendable diligence, Brother. Financial restraints, as you are aware, have led to the abandonment of our plans for stone vaulting in the south transept. Thanks be to God, I have now given instructions to Master Kenrick to remedy the situation and, as one thing leads to another, he will be able to make vaults for the north transept, too. Indeed, he has spoken to me with enthusiasm about incorporating miniature shafted arcading there, which I am sure will be a delight to the eye."

With jaundiced expression, Thurgot said through clenched teeth,

"I am sure it will, Your Grace, for Master Kenrick is a gifted mason. God has favoured us with his presence in Durham. However, surely some funds can be diverted for the needs of the brothers? The people, when they think of Durham cathedral also, rightly, think of the monks who continue the tradition Cuthbert started at Melrose and Lindisfarne."

Bishop Ranulf was losing patience and it showed in his testy reply,

"That may well be so, Prior. Buy the brethren a new bucket. They must make do with the well in the cloister—a commodity I believe you were responsible for creating."

"A new bucket!"

The Prior could not help but raise his voice in outrage. There was a notable difference between the monks having access to a laver with running water next to the refectory and the discomfort of fetching water up from the well and carrying it to the washbasins.

"Ay, you vaunt the simple life of the hermit-saint and yet lament a minor vexation, which is no more than a small hardship to be borne in the context of the greater glory of the cathedral. The high vault of the north transept requires considerable expense. Master Kenrick tells me he will have to solve the not indifferent technical problem of the vaulting by using a completely new technique of diagonal ribbing. There, what do you think of that? The mason's genius soars whilst you bore me with mundane problems of water supply! The monks are not without water. Once we have completed the cathedral, they shall have their laver."

Prior Thurgot had listened to this increasingly aggressive speech without undue annoyance but now, patiently, he pointed out,

"If his Grace would deign to visit the cloister, he would see that we already have a laver in the south-west corner but although we have identified springs on the west side of the Wear, we need to buy lead piping to bring a supply by skilful use of gravity to the lavers, the kitchen, bakehouse and maybe even a future brewhouse. Surely, Your Grace can see that the present system of the well supplying water to a cistern, with its standpipe, manually filled by the brothers, is outdated and inadequate? I beg Your Grace to reconsider."

The prelate curled his lip, he had the satisfaction of knowing that whatever the monk chose to say, he would win this argument because his behind-the-scenes work had paid off. With what relish would he deliver his surprise! But first, he must weary the prior with his superior argumentation.

"Enough, Thurgot! I have explained my priorities and have not yet mentioned the nave. The plans are grandiose and require every penny we can raise. The main arcades consist of *three* double-bays and a single western bay. *You* tell me where the money must come from to complete it."

"The diocese has many churches and estates that pay tithes into Durham's coffers. The monks do not claim these incomes, but the offerings to the saint are a different matter! We believe that a small part can be spared for the welfare of the brethren."

The time had come and he delivered the blow with a measured, subtle tone, disguising his glee,

"You have my answer, Your Grace."

"*Your Grace*, to me?"

"Indeed! Congratulations! Did you not know that the king at the request of the rulers of Scotland has appointed you, Thurgot, to the see of St Andrews? I am sure that with your outstanding abilities you will make an excellent bishop. With my blessing, you may leave as soon as you are ready. Never fear, dear brother, one day the brethren here will have their water pipe. Meanwhile, it is no longer *your* problem."

Thurgot looked aghast at the bishop of Durham. He had been aware for over a year that this day might come, but now that it had arrived, it had taken him by surprise and left him speechless.

Bereft of speech was how the prelate preferred the troublesome monk and he looked smug and his voice became mellifluous, as he handed the letter of appointment to the prior.

"My dear Brother in Christ, this is a long-overdue reward for your organisational abilities and irreprehensible conduct. I wish you every success. Please send me your sub-prior, for I desire to test his suitability to assume your duties."

Although his head was reeling at the devastating news, Thurgot collected himself swiftly to sustain his friend,

"Your Grace, I can wholeheartedly speak in favour of Brother Aldwine as my successor. He is a humble man and well-loved by his brethren."

"Ay, ay. I shall bear your recommendation in mind, Prior, but as Abbot, I must make my own decisions"

On his way out of the bishop's residence, Thurgot wondered how he had offended God. His life had been dedicated to the resurrection of the work of Saint Cuthbert. Where was the sense of going to Scotland? He had not strolled far, lost in thought before his musings led him to ask a more pertinent question. What had been the point in his fleeing to Norway? And yet, it had brought him here. God certainly moved in mysterious ways. He sighed and accepted his lot. He did not have any possessions to pack, just a copy of the Gospels that he had acquired here in Durham, so it was a question of saying his farewells and going to Scotland.

The first to know must be Aldwine, also because he had to send him to the bishop. So, he found his friend and said,

"I am leaving my office here as prior to take up a new position as bishop of St Andrews. You must hasten to Bishop Ranulf, Brother, who wishes to ascertain your worthiness to succeed me. Take my advice and make no mention either of Cuthbert or our water problem if you wish to be prior. I have made my recommendations in your favour."

They embraced, exchanged farewells and Thurgot offered further counsel. Separating from Aldwine, he gathered the brothers in the chapter house, by tolling the assembly bell and amid general dismay and head-shaking, related the facts and he took his leave of the abbey. His most important greeting he kept for last, for his dearest friend, who, he knew would take his departure very badly, so to stall and collect his thoughts, he went to his cell and picked up his bible and a small wooden wall cross, which were all he possessed in this world.

Hesitating on the threshold of where the western end of the cathedral would be built, he gazed down along the uncompleted nave and gasped. The visual effect hitherto achieved by Kenrick took his breath away. The columns with their flutes and lozenges offset by the alternating red and black zig-zagged piers with their carved capitals, combined to create a beauty the like of which he had never seen. Was Bishop Ranulf correct after all to give precedence to the construction of the cathedral? But what were Durham and the Cuthbert legacy without the monks? If Ranulf Flambard continued to neglect the brothers there would be fewer vocations entering the monastery and gradually it would decline. Pushing these thoughts aside with a sigh, he strode in among the building rubble and found Kenrick advising a young mason, who was carving a man with two dogs hunting a stag.

"What does this portray, Master?"

Kenrick turned and greeted the Prior with a grin.

"You should ask the bishop, he suggested it. It's a saint who converted to Christianity when he saw an apparition of Jesus appear between the horns of a stag he was hunting. That's what he told me.

"Ah, of course, that would be St Eustace, wouldn't it?"

The master mason chortled and shrugged his huge shoulders,

"I'm only a poor builder, so how would I know? There are so many bloo—blessed saints," when he had lived and worked elsewhere with the monks his language had been acceptable but with the need here to bellow orders at a host of labourers it had deteriorated, "I can't be expected to know them all! Now you're a priest, I mean a monk—"

"This time you are right, my friend, I know I've corrected you on that score many times, but last year, I was ordained. God has seen fit to make of me a bishop."

Kenrick looked surprised, scratched his grey hair, looked puzzled and said,

"The bishop didn't tell me he was leaving. He was here only yesterday and said nothing about it."

"Likely because he's going nowhere, Kenrick."

Realisation dawned on the dusty face of his friend, followed by a mournful expression,

"It's what you told me some time ago, isn't it? You're away to Scotland."

"Ay, that's it."

The giant mason put his arm around the monk's shoulder,

"Come with me," he steered the confused monk out of the cathedral and they walked, arms linked, downhill past the castle until they came to a stable.

Kenrick propelled him inside and in his booming voice called for the stablemaster. A bandy-legged rotund fellow with rosy cheeks and very little fair hair appeared and grumbled,

"Who's that shouting and bawling? You'll disturb the horses. Oh, it's you, Master Kenrick. Have you come for your Smoca?"

"Ay, that's right. I paid for stabling this month, so I don't owe you aught."

"I'll just saddle her and fetch her then, she's a sweet-natured beast."

The former prior stared at his friend,

"What are we doing here, Kenrick?"

The mason again rested his muscular arm around the monk's slight shoulders,

"Isn't it clear? I'm giving you a parting gift. I'm not having you tramp up to Scotland. It's not fitting for a bishop."

"But you love your horse. I can't possibly take her."

"Oh, you can, and you will. I've no time to ride her any more, anyway, yon bloo—blessed cathedral takes my every waking moment..."

His voice trailed away as the stablemaster came leading the dappled grey mare by its reins.

Thurgot passed through many emotions as his friend consigned the horse to him. He could scarcely see his friend as his eyes welled with tears of... what? Gratitude, love, or sorrow? All three most likely. There were no adequate words, so he mounted the mare and with a click of his tongue and a tap of his heel, they moved slowly out of the stable.

When he looked back at Durham, the first thing that struck him was the stunted cathedral dominating the hill. Bishop Ranulf was right, he had to admit, the building needed its western towers as planned by Kenrick and backed by Flambard. With majestic towers, it would be a sight of great beauty on the heights in the curve of the river amid the rising greenery on the sides of the crag. It was becoming a truly worthy resting place for the greatest of Northumbria's saints. Had he, Thurgot, a wanderer from Lindsey, been an irreproachable servant of the servants of Cuthbert? Leaving them now, in a moment of their need, for the unknown adventure as bishop of a see he knew next to nothing about made his heart ache.

The Queen of Scotland, Margaret was a devout woman raised first, in exile in the bosom of the most Catholic court of Hungary, then, brought home by Edward the Confessor, another deeply religious monarch. With the unruly Malcolm, a widower, she had achieved wonders and he was devoted to her and indulgent of her deeply-held spiritual views. That she had pressed for Thurgot to come and reform the see of St Andrews was a great honour as was her desire to entrust the education of her children to him. Aware of the esteem accorded him, Thurgot had misgivings and still only an hour away from Durham, wished only to return there. Making good progress, he blessed Kenrick for his kindness and patted the dappled grey mare, which whinnied and tossed her head.

To try to forget his inner torment and praise God instead of brooding on his lot, he reflected on the significance of dappling. Smoca was a beautiful dappled grey mare—the Almighty in his wisdom had made many creatures and plants variegated to add to the magnificence of His Creation. He listed them in his mind: the stippled hues of the trout, the linnet's breast, the orange and red sky at sunset, freckles on the milkmaid's face, the brindled cow she milked, sunlight filtering through the forest treetops and dappling a glade. Pleasure at thoughts of beauty uplifted him and in his rich, mellow voice began to sing David's psalm to the majesty of creation:

'O Lord, our Lord,
how majestic is your name in all the earth!
You have set your glory
above the heavens.'

His eyes roved over the countryside without observing that the landscape was dappled, too. Absorbed in remembering the words of Psalm 8, he ignored here a fallow field, there a stretch of golden barley, beside another of green-topped vegetables. Yet, his heart sang and he exorcised the futility of his earlier depression with redoubled volume to his singing. Remember this day, Thurgot scolded himself; when melancholy descends, seek out a dappled flower or visit Smoca in her stall—or better, ride her out into the countryside. He finished the second verse of the psalm with a flourish and promised to write one himself one day, in praise of pied things.

> '...all flocks and herds,
> and the animals of the wild,
> the birds in the sky,
> and the fish in the sea,
> all that swim the paths of the seas.'

As if in response to his cheerful singing, Smoca was cantering just short of a gallop. He thought about the poor creature. They were facing a journey of sixty-five leagues and, even with the ferry across the Forth founded by Queen Margaret for the use of pilgrims on their way to St Andrews, she would need drink, food and rest and so would he. If he wanted to spare the horse, which he did, he was contemplating a six-day journey, at least. He had very little money and so, he would need to find charitable lodgings along the way.

Only the first day gave him a problem and he was becoming so desperate to find a place for the night that he considered straying from the direct route. Instead, he prayed to St Cuthbert for guidance and at a place called Widdrington, he obtained directions from the priest to an abandoned hermit's cell. Thurgot was happy to make do with the most rudimentary lodgings and this one provided him and his beast with a freshwater stream. The friendly cleric who had mentioned the cell supplied him with bread and cheese; Smoca fed on lush grass near the hermitage and so, they resumed their wanderings refreshed the next day, and in Bamburgh found a stable with the monks and a bed for Thurgot. The abbot came to find his illustrious visitor and on learning of his travels told him how and where to break it for the next few nights, giving him a few coins and food from the kitchen for the ride.

Within three days, he was in his new residence in St Andrews and the Durham chapter of his life was well and truly closed.

TWENTY-TWO

DURHAM, NORTHUMBRIA 1114 AD

Although of low birth, when he was a youth Ranulf Flambard stood out amongst the other clerks for his intelligence and good looks. Flambard was a nickname and Archbishop Anselm of Canterbury, who disliked him intensely, told the pope that the epithet came from Ranulf's cruelty, which Anselm likened to a consuming flame. The prelate did not lead an exemplary life: among his sins was a blatant exploitation of nepotism. One of Ranulf's nephews, Ralf, was appointed archdeacon of Northumberland since Ranulf ignored his predecessor's instructions that the prior would also be archdeacon. He ensured that many members of his family were granted remunerative positions such as sheriff or holders of important fiefs. But nepotism was perhaps the least of his transgressions as the bishop kept concubines and had sons by them.

His colourful past included arrest by the new king, Henry I, for embezzlement, and subsequent imprisonment in the Tower of London on 15 August 1100. His custodian, William de Mandeville, allowed the prisoner to escape through the window of his cell by a rope which accomplices had smuggled to him in a flagon of wine. Ranulf plied the guards with the drink, and after they were drunk and asleep, climbed down the cord to flee. His friends had arranged a ship to transport Ranulf, some of the bishop's treasure, and the bishop's mother to Normandy.

Undoubtedly a resourceful collector of taxes both for himself and for the king, Orderic the chronicler described Ranulf's career as *addicted to feasts and carousals and lusts; cruel and ambitious, prodigal to his adherents, but rapacious in seizing the goods of other men;* whilst Archbishop Anselm of Canterbury wrote to Pope Paschal II, while Ranulf was in exile, portraying Ranulf as *a rent collector of the worst possible reputation* and *a plunderer of the rich, destroyer of the poor.* Nonetheless, before he died in 1128, he ensured that Durham cathedral was all but completed thanks to his unscrupulous accumulation of funds.

The young and alluring niece of his mistress Aelfgifu paid her aunt a visit in 1114. As soon as Ranulf set eyes upon her, he wanted her for himself. Why not make this delightful girl his concubine, like her aunt?

The same girl, a virtuous maid, was strolling along a corridor, somewhat lost in the bishop's residence, when he spotted her through an open door. Moving stealthily like a preying lynx, he crept up behind her, wrapped an arm around her waist and clapped a hand over her mouth so that she would not alert the household by screaming. Drawing her easily into the room, he closed the heavy door with a shove of his foot. Removing his hand from her face, he used the gentlest tone he could muster,

"Do not be afraid my sweet, it is I, the bishop. Since the moment I saw you, I realised that the angels had sent you to me to provide me with love and comfort. In return, I shall bestow jewels and finery upon you. You will want for nothing and be seated by my side at the high table. All I require of you," he stroked her breast delicately, "is a little affection in return. Just like your aunt Aelfgifu has given me. You will have seen how happy she is in my household? What do you say, my beauty?" He took her hand and slowly led her into his bedchamber.

Theodora, this religious and virtuous maid, looked at him with wild eyes, but she was possessed of considerable intelligence and so, she suppressed her fear and desire to flee.

"I say, I consent, Your Grace, but with just one condition."

"Name it."

"I am shy and cannot bear the thought of anyone finding us at our lovemaking. I beg you, allow me to bolt the door for privacy."

"Of course, my love, see to it at once."

Theodora hurried to the stout door, but instead of bolting it on the inside, slipped through and slid the bolt home on the outside. In vain, the irritated prelate thrust his weight against it, hammered and cursed. Nobody heard or found him.

Flustered, heart pounding, Theodora hastened to her aunt and recounted the tale of her misadventure. Aelfgifu reassured her and settled her in a comfortable chamber, placing a guard on the door, saying,

"Not even the bishop may enter the room, do you understand?"

She hastened to the prelate's bed-chamber and, unbolting the door, found him, brooding, stretched out on his bed. She, too, was an intelligent woman, so made no accusation but rapidly disrobed and, naked, clambered upon him. Only when their carnal desires were satisfied and the bishop lay spent on his back, did she lean over and threaten him.

"Can you imagine how easy it would be for a woman to slay a man as he lies recovering from his lovemaking? Attempt to rape my niece again and I cannot vow that my love for you will not lead me to avenge her in a fit of passion. Oh, my sweet love, am I not able to assuage your desires?" Her kisses began low on his belly until he was aroused again and promised eagerly never more to lay hands upon the maid. Aelfgifu, however, used her hands on him and her threat was soon forgiven although not forgotten.

Ranulf was a man who harboured rancour but this time, it was not directed against Aelfgifu but her niece. As soon as the girl's parents arrived in Durham, to exact revenge on her, he brokered a marriage between her and a young nobleman named Beorhtred. Theodora's parents readily agreed, but Theodora did not, because of her vow to remain a virgin. Her parents, annoyed at being thwarted, arranged for Beorhtred to have access to her room, only to discover next morning that the two had spent the night discussing religious matters. The next evening, Theodora hid behind a tapestry whilst Beorhtred searched for her in vain. Word soon spread of the maid's plight and a hermit named Eadwine, with the blessing of Ranulf's ecclesiastical rival and foe, the Archbishop of Canterbury, dressed her in male clothing and helped her to escape the palace. Eadwine then took her to stay with an anchoress, Alfwen, at Flamstead who hid her from her family, changing her name to Christina.

Foiled in his amorous ambitions and attempt at revenge, Bishop Ranulf redirected his energies to the construction of the cathedral. With this in mind, he strolled the short distance from his residence to consult about progress with the master mason. He stopped momentarily once more to admire the chevrons over the west door— sculpted two years before. Wandering into the nave as far as the crossing, he looked up at the recently completed vaulting and allowed himself a smile of satisfaction. A labourer rested a wheelbarrow laden with wet cement so that he could bow to the eminent visitor. The bishop nodded, smiled and followed the barrow, wobbling under the weight of mortar, into the aisle. Kenrick was working on an arcade, checking the perfect verticality of his stonework.

"Master, a word, if it is convenient. Forgive me, I know you are busy."

"Never too busy not to spare you my time, Your Grace."

The prelate smiled thinly. He wished to be remembered for his great contribution to the cathedral but he also yearned to see it finished in his lifetime. His gaze roved over the mason and he considered his age. The man was a phenomenon. The grey whiskers and hair, slowly turning white told him that he had passed his allotted three-score-and-ten and, yet, he still managed to scale ladders and lift weights. But with all the grace of God, he could not continue indefinitely. His energy must be safeguarded like a precious jewel because it was his brain that Bishop Ranulf cherished. Who but this genius would have conceived of so many new and successful solutions? Others throughout Europe would copy Kenrick's schemes, of that he had no doubt.

"Master Mason, I desire that you conserve your energy for planning design and hastening the building towards completion. Let other and younger men do the heavy work and the scaling of scaffolding and ladders."

"But, Your Grace, if I want a job done to perfection, perforce I have to do it myself."

"Master Kenrick, do not disobey me. You are too valuable to me and I wish to see the building completed as you do. I have come here today to talk about the towers. The sooner they are built, the happier I will be.

"Begging your pardon, Your Excellency, but we cannot build the towers until the aisles are roofed and the south transept vaulted. That transept's given me sleepless nights, ay, that it has."

"How so?"

"Well, to vault it, I shall have to cut the central clerestory pier to allow for ribs. And I reckon the whole structure will have to be supported from small tunnel vaults over the passageway. Now, tell me, what time will I have to erect the western towers? I have roughed out a plan for them and a central tower. Please come to the lodge, Your Grace and I'll show you."

As they ambled outside, the bishop adapted his stride to that of the elderly mason, who kept turning and delaying as if visualising the edifice with the towers constructed.

Inside the lodge, he cleared a space on a bench and unrolled and flattened a parchment.

"See here, Your Grace, these are the western towers. Now, I figured that being as the cathedral is on a crag and to be seen from below by approaching pilgrims, they will need to have a height of one hundred and fifty feet. The central tower, even more important, should reach to two hundred feet. Either that or they'll all be lost from view."

"In our present world, Master Mason, I cannot face the expense these heights would entail. You will have to re-size. One day, my successors, God willing, will be able to afford the cost of the dimensions you suggest. Halve them, my friend, and since I take your point about visibility from below, cap your towers with steeples."

Kenrick's mouth dropped open and his eyes darkened with fury,

"You cannot mean what you say. You'd ruin the whole effect, the beauty of the cathedral, by sticking dwarf towers and steeples on top!"

The bishop's eyes betrayed his anger.

"Do not dare contradict me, old man! It is an order and what's more, I want these towers finished by the end of next year at the latest, understood?"

The prelate did not wait for a reply but strode out of the lodge towards the castle with nary a backwards glance, nor, for that matter a sideways one at the cathedral.

Kenrick sank onto a three-legged stool and held his head in his hands. Careless of whether the bishop was out of earshot, he moaned,

"May the bastard rot in a bog! Halve them: damned if I will!" His giant fist slammed painfully onto his thigh, "Steeples! I'll roast in Hell first! And all by the end of next year— impossible!" He leapt to his feet, groaned, clutched his head and his face contorted, saliva foamed at the corner of his mouth, his left arm dangled uselessly and he couldn't reach out to prevent himself from falling by grasping the table. He tried to call for help but he could no longer form words. He crashed to the floor. Lying there, he tried to recall his best friend's name but his brain betrayed him, he could not remember. He realised dimly that he would never see the cathedral, *his* church, completed. Moments later, Master Kenrick, Master of the Chevron, died of apoplexy in the lodge, aged seventy-five. The greatest part of the work on the Norman edifice was done and would live on for centuries as a recognised masterpiece in tribute to him, the Saxon mason.

Another builder found him and sent Faruin, who ran to inform the bishop. The prelate came with unction and as with many of his actions, he transgressed since the last rites may not be given after death. Ignoring the rules of the Church, partly to act out a scene of respect for the cowed and shocked workforce gathered there and partly out of guilt because he suspected his contribution to the mason's demise, he proceeded to anoint the corpse. Master Kenrick was buried in the monk's graveyard behind the monastery. There, Prior Aldwine conducted the service and had Kenrick been able to comment, he would have said the prior was the best person to do so in the absence of Thurgot.

TWENTY-THREE

ST ANDREWS, EAST LOTHIAN, 1114-15 AD

IN THE SPACE OF A FEW HOURS, BISHOP THURGOT RECEIVED TWO letters: one brought tears to his eyes and the other provoked anger and frustration. The first, from his former sub-prior, now, Prior Aldwine, informed him of the death of his old friend, Kenrick. Fighting back his sorrow, Thurgot hastened to the chapel and sank to his knees to thank God for the life of the master mason, without whose intervention, he, the bishop, would have been drowned many decades ago. Together, as firm friends, they had built the magnificent cathedral in Durham to the glory of the Almighty and now, he thought bitterly, he had to start over again. St Andrews boasted no cathedral, just a primitive reliquary church and although thanks to the efforts of Queen Margaret, pilgrims had begun to worship at the reliquary of St Andrew, he could not construct a cathedral without the financial backing of someone as wealthy and vigorous as the late lamented William of St Calais.

Begging forgiveness of the Lord for allowing his problems to distract him from his eulogy to Kenrick, he finished his devotions and returned to the exasperations of his daily life in Scotland. Even, some minutes of intense prayer reiterated to him the true nature of his suffering. Old, and weary of dealing with earthly powers, kings, archbishops, and confraternities, he wished to serve only one heavenly Master.

King Alexander had pressed for him to be appointed as bishop of St Andrews and primate of Scotland. He had known Thurgot from his infancy and knew the support he had given his mother, Margaret and of his excellent work s prior and archdeacon at Durham. The king wanted Thurgot to help reform the Scottish church so that it would be in line with the rest of western Christendom. Not even the king realised from what a poisoned chalice he was asking his former mentor to drink.

The see of St Andrews had been subject to control by the archbishops of York since 1072 and Thurgot immediately on appointment was flung into a cauldron boiling over with disaccord. He wished to maintain the supremacy of York, but the king preferred the more distant authority of Canterbury and pressed Thurgot to strive for independence from the hegemony of the archbishop of York.

Owing to this controversy, his consecration had been delayed for two years until 1109. In addition to political wrangling and the lack of a cathedral, he discovered the knotty problem of the Culdees. Rather like the old days of the Cuthbert community, the Culdees were a distinct body at St Andrews and lived in families, where they followed their traditional forms of worship. Thurgot was faced with an impossible task. How could he introduce his beloved Benedictine monasticism without any dedicated monks and in a place that had been without a bishop for sixteen years? Moreover, the Culdees occupied many of the Scottish monasteries and none had adopted the Benedictine Rule.

Trudging out of the chapel, Thurgot sighed heavily, feeling the weight of the world on his shoulders. At his advanced age, he had recently surpassed three-score-and-four winters, how could he reconcile these factions—the king, the archbishop of York, the Culdees—each and every one seeking to make him forsake the truths he had lived by? The stress was making him ill. King Alexander sent messengers to Pope Paschal II asking him to write to Thurgot about such matters as the fasting known as the Ember-days, the giving of the Eucharist to children, and confessing to priests.

The pope issued a missive to the clergy and laity, demanding they commit to Thurgot:

'our fellow bishop...among the wiser among you.'

He then wrote another to Thurgot and sent with it a book of excerpts from canon law, referring him to rulings of fifth-century popes. This was the second letter of the day, the one that provoked anger and frustration. The Holy Father could not understand the intricacies of his situation, sitting so far away in beatitude in his summer residence among the hills at Civita Castellana.

Feeling alone, inadequate and exasperated, the bishop shredded the letter and came to a radical decision.

I must prepare to go to Rome and consult with Paschal in person. I'll make him understand my plight and, God willing, he will let me stay and pass the rest of my life under his wise and holy counsel.

Later that day, Thurgot wrote to the king, begging his permission to sail for Rome. The reply was swift in reaching St Andrews and equally as brusque:

"We forbid it. The journey to Rome is long and dangerous, and quite unsuitable for you, our beloved friend, at your age."

Rather more than concern for his old tutor, King Alexander considered that the long pilgrimage would further delay the changes he wished to introduce. They were already long overdue because of the deferment of Thurgot's consecration for two years owing to his obedience to York.

Continuing weeks of vexation and discontent culminated for Thurgot in February in the death of Thomas, the archbishop of York, a man Thurgot respected and could rely upon. The new archbishop-elect was in opposition to the king of England and the archbishop of Canterbury. The simple Benedictine monk, now wearing the guise of bishop's vestments— moreover, unwanted— found himself involved in a tussle between King Alexander, Archbishop Anselm and Bishop

Ranulf Flambard of Durham, over the metropolitan supremacy of York over St Andrews. His soul was troubled.

How can I tolerate these earthly princes when all I want is to live for Christ, my spiritual prince?

At the height of his disheartenment came a summons from the king. Alexander had the Culdee monastery at Scone rebuilt and at the king's command, Bishop Thurgot was to dedicate the church to the Holy Trinity. Not that he could refuse this engagement, which was in honour of the king's victory over the men of Moray, but he found some enthusiasm because Augustinian canons were invited to settle into the monastery from Yorkshire. They would not have been his perfect choice but pleased him better than the Culdees. He was not to know it, but as many observed at the ceremony, the once authoritative bishop seemed frail and old— it was to be his last public engagement. During the rest of 1114, his health declined and broke under the anxieties he was enduring.

Maybe St Cuthbert will heal me. I must away to his shrine.

Given his enfeebled state, in the following year, the king gave him licence to stay for a while in Durham. The joyous thought that he could return to Durham was sufficient to renew his strength to face the journey and refusing all wheeled transport, set off on the faithful Smoca in June 1115. He had a list in his mind of what he wanted to do before he died. The first of these was to break his ride at Monkwearmouth, where he arrived on 28 June. The place held special importance for him, for there, he had been clothed by Prior Aldwyn in a monastic habit for the first time, forty years previously. There, too, he celebrated his last Mass.

Setting out for Durham, he proceeded at once to the stables and returned Smoca to her former stall. Then, with his energy no more than a dim spark, he visited the saint's shrine and, heart swelling with contentment, prayed for the soul of the mason who had built this glorious monument. He studiously avoided talking with the new master mason but, nonetheless, found the strength to bless him from a distance before seeking Prior Aldwine and imploring him to lead him to Kenrick's grave. The prior, shocked and dismayed at his old friend's decline, realised that the bishop was near death and whilst Thurgot lowered his protesting bones to kneel, murmuring incoherently beside the grave of his lifelong friend, the prior hurried away to make arrangements for a comfortable bed in a private cell in the monastery for the illustrious guest.

"I told you, all those years ago that God had great plans for you," Thurgot spoke to the grassy mound, looking around with difficulty at the bulk of the cathedral. It still lacked its towers but he had noted the completed nave and the roofed aisles on entering to visit the shrine. The beauty of the master's work had stolen away what little breath he had to spare. His heart had rejoiced at the chevron decoration on the springing in the nave; it had produced a smile at its significance.

"I noticed it, old friend, I truly did! I refer to your signature in the nave—my dearest Master of the Chevron!"

Tottering to his feet with the indispensable aid of his staff, Thurgot, knowing his end was drawing near, hobbled into the cloister. Aldwine met him and conducted him to his bed-chamber.

"Here, dear Brother is where the angels will collect my soul when the Lord decides the time is right. Praise God that I can die near the body of Saint Cuthbert."

Prior Aldwine gazed sorrowfully at the bright febrile eyes and the heated brow of his friend and fought back the mendacious platitudes of comfort on the tip of his tongue.

"Ay, the saint is but a hundred paces away, dear Brother."

The gentle smile told him that, on reflection, he had found the right words. July came and went, but Thurgot remained in his bed, passing from one febrile attack to another. During this period, despite his increasing weakness, he was able to share his knowledge with distinguished visitors. Among these, Thurstan, archbishop-elect of York, came to learn as much as he could of the subtleties involved in Anglo-Scottish relationships. An old foe, Bishop Ranulf, visited, too, but bringing genuine respect and fondness to his bedside. Although the bishop of St Andrews survived July and most of August, his flesh had fallen away and his voice become so weak that listeners struggled to hear him but on 31 August 1115, the few people in the room distinctly heard him say,

"His dwelling is in peace and his habitation in Zion."

They were the last words he uttered before his soul left his wasted body.

When they were referred to Bishop Flambard, that bishop of debatable morals, nonetheless one knowledgeable enough, declared,

"Psalm 76, verse two. I wonder why—"

The bishop stood lost in thought, pondering whether Thurgot had been comparing *their* cathedral to the chosen abode of the Lord.

THE END

POSTSCRIPT

"Durham Cathedral is justly recognised as the culminating achieve-ment of the Norman Romanesque school in England." (John Bilson, *Durham Cathedral*)

"...Its master played a leading part in the age of the first Enlighten-ment." (Jean Bony, *The Stonework Planning of the First Durham Master*)

"The character of the work at Durham changed so little between its inception in 1093 and the completion of the nave in 1133 that the visitor, after entering the church by the North portal and sitting down in the nave to abandon himself to his first impressions, can be certain that it is essentially at the design of the first great master that he is looking." (Nikolaus Pevsner, *The Cathedrals of England*)

The exquisite irony of Durham Cathedral is that it is regarded as a Norman masterpiece and yet, many architectural experts agree that the unknown first master was most likely a Saxon, given the many Anglo-Saxon traits in his work.

His genius can be measured in the revolutionary features he introduced and it is indisputable that he anticipated and blazed the trail for the subsequent marvellous Gothic explosion in Western Europe. Below, I'd like to point out some of the novelties he introduced.

Firstly, while most English churches of the time were built at least partially of wood, Durham Cathedral was to be entirely made of stone and since Roman times, nobody had built without at least incorporating wood, so it was an ambitious project. Romanesque buildings were entirely made of stone, but they could only support that much weight by being thick, heavy, and with very few windows. The bishop of Durham wanted a more spacious and lighter interior. The master mason erected columns built into opposite walls would extend into the ceiling, arching up and meeting at a point in the middle. By creating a long corridor of these pointed arches, the ceiling could be taller and wider, allowing for more interior space.

In this building the three main innovations of the revolutionary Gothic style come together: pointed arches, ribbed vaults, and flying buttresses, which are hidden above the aisle vaults and anticipate the later external ones elsewhere. The great German expert E. Gall went so far as to characterise them as 'one of the first realisations of a fully structural way of thinking.' So, Durham Cathedral can proudly boast being the proto-Gothic progenitor of High Gothic architecture.

The ribbed vaulting dispersed weight into the columns, making most of the wall between the columns redundant. The mason realised that he could take out parts of the wall and insert windows instead, allowing for far more natural light.

The design of Durham calls for a compact three-storey elevation constructed with unvaulted galleries and massive walls. The walls at Durham are constructed in the double-wall technique so that the structure is inwardly stabilised through the bulk of its walls (each 2 metres thick) and has no need or any auxiliary buttressing.

Durham displays the first use of chevrons in England (except perhaps for the dormitory at Canterbury) but soon other masons followed suit. Underneath the windows all around the inside of the cathedral is the continuous arcade of interlocking arches, the earliest in Britain. There is a theory that out of this solution developed the idea of the pointed or ogival arch.

————

Twelfth-century construction work:

After the death of Prior Thurgot, building on the Cathedral continued to progress as follows:

1125-33 The walls of the Nave completed. The West towers were halted until a gable was built at the west end.

1133-35 the choir screen was created.

1133-40 The chapter house was completed using rib vaulting with keeled mouldings.

The walls of the nave were erected up to its vault.

1150 the dormitory was completed.

1160s West end galilee built

1190 Shrine for the Venerable Bede created in the galilee.

————

Bishop Ranulf Flambard survived Thurgot and it was he who ordained Thurstan, the archbishop-elect of York, as a priest in 1115, although Thurstan had to wait for consecration as bishop for another four years. Ranulf attended the council of Rheims in 1119 held by Pope Callixtus II. In 1125 John of Crema, the papal legate to England, visited Durham to investigate charges of scandal against the bishop. Some later chroniclers told the story that the legate was much taken with Ranulf's niece, and after sleeping with the girl, took no action on the charges against Ranulf. This is colourful, but probably untrue. Bishop Ranulf died in 1128 and whilst his reputation was very poor in the Middle Ages, modern historians consider that he was an able administrator and financier. Durham Cathedral certainly reaped the benefits of his financial skills.

Dear reader,

We hope you enjoyed reading *The Master Of The Chevron.* Please take a moment to leave a review, even if it's a short one. Your opinion is important to us.

Discover more books by John Broughton at

https://www.nextchapter.pub/authors/john-broughton

Want to know when one of our books is free or discounted? Join the newsletter at

http://eepurl.com/bqqB3H

Best regards,

John Broughton and the Next Chapter Team

ABOUT THE AUTHOR

John Broughton was born in Cleethorpes Lincolnshire UK in 1948: just one of the post-war baby boom. After attending grammar school and studying to the sound of Bob Dylan he went to Nottingham University and studied Medieval and Modern History (Archaeology subsidiary). The subsidiary course led to one of his greatest academic achievements: tipping the soil content of a wheelbarrow from the summit of a spoil heap on an old lady hobbling past the dig. He did actually many different jobs while living in Radcliffe-on-Trent, Leamington, Glossop, the Scilly Isles, Puglia and Calabria. They include teaching English and History, managing a Day Care Centre, being a Director of a Trade Institute and teaching university students English. He even tried being a fisherman and a flower picker when he was on St. Agnes island, Scilly. He has lived in Calabria since 1992 where he settled into a long-term job at the University of Calabria teaching English. No doubt his lovely Calabrian wife Maria stopped him being restless. His two kids are grown up now, but he wrote books for them when they were little. Hamish Hamilton and then Thomas Nelson published 6 of these in England in the 1980s. They are now out of print. He's a granddad now and happily the parents wisely named his grandson Dylan. He decided to take up writing again late in his career. When teaching and working as a translator you don't really have time for writing. As soon as he stopped the translation work, he resumed writing in 2014. The fruit of that decision was his first historical novel, *The Purple Thread* followed by *Wyrd of the Wolf*. Both are set in his favourite Anglo-Saxon period.

His third and fourth novels, a two-book set, are *Saints and Sinners* and its sequel *Mixed Blessings* set on the cusp of the eighth century in Mercia and Lindsey. A fifth *Sward and Sword* will is about the great Earl Godwine. Creativia Publishing have released *Perfecta Saxonia* and *Ulf's Tale* about King Aethelstan and King Cnut's empire respectively. In May 2019, they published *In the Name of the Mother*, a sequel to *Wyrd of the Wolf*. Creativia/Next Chapter also published *Angenga* a time-travel novel linking the ninth century to the twenty-first. This novel inspired John Broughton's latest venture, a series of six stand-alone novels about psychic investigator Jake Conley, whose retrocognition takes him back to Anglo-Saxon times. Next Chapter Publishing scheduled the first of these, *Elfrid's Hole* for publication at the end of October 2019. The second, is *Red Horse Vale* and the third, *Memory of a Falcon*. The fourth is *The Snape Ring*. The fifth, *Pinions of Gold* is on pre-sale on Amazon. The last of the series *The Serpent Wand* is also under consideration by the same publisher.

The author's latest project was a trilogy of 'pure' Anglo-Saxon novels about Saint Cuthbert. The first is *Heaven in a Wild Flower, The Horse-thegn* is the second and the third is *The Master of the Chevron.*